B

the
Best Book
Bible Companion for the Home

————————

BY
JAMES EDSON WHITE

————————

SOUTHERN PUBLISHING ASSOCIATION

Fort Worth, Texas   Nashville, Tennessee   Atlanta, Georgia

PREFACE

THIS little book is divided into two parts. The First Department is the children's very own. It is for them to study under the guidance of teacher, mother, brother, or sister. It has been prepared with great care by one who has had many years' experience as a teacher of children.

The Second Department is for the entertainment of children both young and old. Its lessons are taken from God's Word. While the children are learning to read from the "Easy Lesson" department, let the parents and older brothers and sisters read to them the Bible stories which follow, showing and explaining to them the beautiful pictures which accompany them. Lessons taught in this manner will never be forgotten.

To Teachers and Parents.

God speaks to us through His Word, by His Spirit, and through nature. By interesting children in nature, which is all about them, it is hoped they will find pleasure in studying God's open book, and thus be led to love and study His written Word.

Blackboard Teaching.—The crayon and the blackboard are very essential in the work with children. Let the first lessons be given in script from the blackboard. The simple sentences may be drawn from the child by questioning. Then tell the child that you will write what he has said. Then ask, "Now can you read it?" The lesson should be about some thing which the child can see, and in which he is interested.

For a review lesson, if the idiom, "I see," has been learned, many sentences may be made by drawing the objects, as "I see a *" (here draw a leaf or some other object). Use the idioms, "I have," "This is," etc., in the same way. The earlier lessons in this book[5] should be largely supplemented from the blackboard in this way, or by variation of the different sentences.

From the first let the children write on the board, where there can be free movement of the arm. Original work should be aimed at from the start. The child soon learns to write the idiom, "I see;" then he is prepared to do original work on the board or on paper. The blackboard work on page 33 is suggestive of what may be done in original work.

Sentence Reading.—The words of a sentence should not be read separately. At first the sentences are short, and the words are soon easily known at sight. Until the thought is known, the sentence should not be read aloud. Hence silent reading should always precede oral reading with children. "Read as you talk," is a good rule.

Writing.—The script capitals and small letters on page 6 are for reference. The letters are not to be written separately, but to be used in words. For practice in writing, use the simple sentences found in the lessons. If written many times, the words will be memorized, and can be used in original work.

Drawing.—Allow free hand drawing. Use outline drawings of objects, as on pages 13 and 49. Lay sticks, then draw them. Provide children with sticks of different lengths. The kindergarten colored sticks are best. They are inexpensive, and can be used in many ways.

Encourage picture illustrations of simple stories. Also the illustration of Bible lessons. Many or all of them may be crude, but thoughts are expressed, and the lesson more deeply impressed.

Reviews.—Observe the suggestion about silent reading first. If the thought is not easily gotten, the words are not familiar—not well learned. The child should use the words many times. As reiteration is the only way in which words are learned through the ear, so it is the only way they are learned through the eye. The use of the blackboard is an invaluable help in making impressions through the eye.

[6]

A	B	C	D	E	F	G	H	I	J
K	L	M	N	O	P	Q	R	S	
	T	U	V	W	X	Y	Z		

a	b	c	d	e	f	g	h	i	j
	k	l	m						
n	o	p	q	r	s	t	u	v	w
	x	y	z						

Letters
[7]

EASY LESSONS.

LESSON ONE.
bird
I see a bird.

Cursive: I see a bird.
I see an apple.

apple
Cursive: I see an apple.
tree
I see a tree.

Cursive: I see a tree.
Is it an apple tree?

Cursive: Is it an
apple tree?
[8]

LESSON TWO
The
two birds
birds.
The
two apples
apples.
The
tree
God made
two birds

apple tree.

the birds.
God made tree tree the trees.
LESSON THREE.
See the
worker bee
bee.
  See the
butterfly
butterfly.
The butterfly has
buttefly wings
wings.
The bee has
bee's wings
wings.
God made them all.

2

LESSON FOUR.
God made the birds.

God made the apples.

God made the apple tree.

God loves the birds.

I love the birds.
Cursive: God made the birds and trees.
LESSON FIVE.
I have box
Cursive: I have a box.
I have tree
Cursive: I have a tree.
John made the box.
God made the tree.
[10]

LESSON SIX.
I have a rose
Cursive: I have a rose.
This is a leaf
Cursive: This is a leaf.
God made the rose and the leaf.
rose   leaf   box   tree
LESSON SEVEN.
See the little bees
cursive: See the little bees.
The bees love the rose.
cursive: The bees love the rose.
bee on rose
The bees are on the rose.
cursive: The bees are on the rose.

bees   little   on   are
[11]

LESSON EIGHT.
rose in colour
See the beautiful rose.

It is red.

I love the beautiful rose.

God made it beautiful.
This leaf is red.
cursive: This leaf is red.
red leaf
green leaf
This leaf is green.

cursive: This leaf is green.
[12]

LESSON NINE.
This is a butterfly.
cursive: This is a butterfly,
He has two wings.
cursive: He has two wings.
The bird has two wings.
cursive: The bird has two wings.
The bird can fly.
cursive: The bird can fly.
The butterfly can fly.
cursive: The butterfly can fly.
I love to see the butterfly.
cursive: I love to see the butterfly.
The butterfly loves the rose.
cursive: The butterfly loves the rose.
He   has   can   butterfly
fly   wings
[13]

LESSON TEN.
cursive: The butterfly has two wings. God made the butterfly. I love the butterfly. The butterfly loves the rose. The bees love the rose. The bees are on the rose. The bee has wings. The bird has wings. The butterfly has beautiful wings. The red rose is beautiful. The grape vine has green leaves.
Leaf, butterfly and boat
Drawing Lesson.
[14]

LESSON ELEVEN.
grapesgrapesgrapesgrapesgrapesgrapes

See this vine.
cursive: See this vine.

It is a grape vine.
cursive: It is a grape vine.

I see the grapes. cursive: I see the grapes.

The grapes grow on the vine.
cursive: The grapes grow on the vine.
Jesus said, I am the true Vine.
[15]

LESSON TWELVE.
cursive: Kittiies, them They Pug dog and two kittens
Do you

kind

care
Do you know me?
cursive: Do you know me?
I love the kitties.
cursive: I love the kitties.

4

I take care of them.
cursive: I take care of them.
I am kind to them.
cursive: I am kind to them.
[16]

LESSON THIRTEEN.
I see the bird.

I love the beautiful birds.

God loves the beautiful birds.

Jesus loves the birds.

The rose is beautiful.

I see three apples.

The apples are on the tree.

I see two birds.

I see the box. John made it.

God made the birds and the trees.

God made the grape vine.

Jesus is the true vine.

The roses and birds are beautiful.

[17]

LESSON FOURTEEN.
Holy Bible.
The Bible is God's holy Book.

Who wrote the Bible?

Holy men wrote the Bible.

God told them what to write.

I
love
God's
holy
Book.
open Bible
Do
you
love
the
Bible?
Can you read the Bible?
Holy Book.
Cursive: God's holy Book.
wrote   write
Cursive: wrote write
Cursive: Can you read? Do you see? What do you see?

5

LESSON FIFTEEN.
Three kittens
Happy little kitties!
Cursive: Happy little kitties!

Who takes care of them?
Cursive: Who takes care of them?

What do they see?
Cursive: What do they see?

Look at their eyes.
Cursive: Look at their eyes.

Are they like yours?
Cursive: Are they like yours?
[19]

LESSON SIXTEEN.
grapesgrapesgrapesgrapes
The Bees.
Mary, see the little bees.

See the bee on the flower.

What is he doing?

He is getting honey.

He is a busy little bee.

Watch him fly to his home.

Do you know where his home is? I can hear the bee buzz.
forms of bee
[20]

LESSON SEVENTEEN.

Bible Verses.
The Lord is good to all.

Praise ye the Lord.

Praise ye Him, sun and moon.

Praise Him, all ye stars of light.

Let them praise the name of the Lord.

harp
O give thanks unto the Lord, for He is good.

Sing praise upon the unto our God.

I will praise the Lord with my whole heart.

[21]

LESSON EIGHTEEN.

grapesgrapesgrapes
This is a family of

They are little black ants.

The ants work.

They live in the ground.

Watch the ants make a house.

The house is made in the ground.

They make rooms in the house.

Watch the ant carry food.

The Bible says, "Watch the ant and be wise."
[22]

LESSON NINETEEN.

rosesrosesrosesrosesroses
See this butterfly
How do you do, pretty butterfly?
I see your beautiful wings.
You love the rose.
Can you get your dinner in the rose?
I love to watch you.
Do you remember when you were a caterpillar?
You are pretty now.
cursive: Pretty butterfly.
Beautiful wings
[23]

LESSON TWENTY.

geese

walk

swim

body
woman at gate with geese
legs

boat

back

dinner
Watch the geese walk.

They can swim better than they can walk.

Their body is the shape of a boat.

Their legs are set far back on the body.

7

Do you know why?

cursive: Watch the geese get their
dinner in the water.
[24]

LESSON TWENTY-ONE.

spider
Here is a
spider.

spider web
This spider
made a web.
The web is his home.

Do you see his home?

rosesroses
Do you see the spider?

The spider loves to work.

Watch a spider make a web.

Do all spiders make webs?

to work   webs
home   his
[25]

LESSON TWENTY-TWO.

Number Story.

number story
[26]

LESSON TWENTY-THREE.

vinevine
Here is a beautiful vine.

It came from a tiny black seed.

It is a morning glory vine.

Do you see the pretty buds?

Can you find a morning glory flower in the evening?

Who gives the morning glory life?

cursive: Morning glory. a tiny black seed. evening.
[27]

LESSON TWENTY-FOUR.

The Flood.

One time God let it rain for many days.

8

The water was very deep. It covered all the earth. All the trees were covered with water.

ark
All the mountains were covered.

In one place the people were safe.

Yes, in the ark.

God had told Noah to make the ark.

Noah loved God. He believed what God told him.

The people did not love God. They did not believe what God told Noah.

They did not believe that God would send a flood.

But the flood came.

Noah and his family were safe in the ark.

[28]

LESSON TWENTY-FIVE.

The Bean's Story. I.

bean planted
Here I am in my warm bed.

John made the box.

He put the dirt into the box.

Mary put me in my bed.

Then she covered me with dirt.

The sun made the bed warm.

The children wanted me to wake up.

They gave me some water.

They said, "This will wake her up."

I love the warm sun and the water.

The children knew this.

children	knew	wanted	water
covered	warm	wake	gave

[29]

LESSON TWENTY-SIX.

The Bean's Story. II.

bean seed with roots
Good morning, children.

9

You see I am awake now.

I am getting out of my white coat.

I put my feet out first.

You call my feet roots.

My roots help me to stand.

Did you know that I have mouths in my roots?

I cannot run about to get my food.

I get food out of the ground.

good	morning		awake	mouths	
white	coat	help	stand	roots	feet

[30]

LESSON TWENTY-SEVEN.

The Bean's Story. III.

bean sprouting
I am glad the children like to watch me.

This morning they can see my tiny leaves.

Shall I tell the children about the mouths in my leaves? I get food out of the air.

My leaves have work to do.

In this, they are like your hands.

I shall have many hands by and by.

shall	hands	leaves	about	air
like	glad	by and by		

[31]

LESSON TWENTY-EIGHT.

The Bean's Story. IV.

bean growing
Do you see my long stem?

I can stand up now.

I shall reach up toward the sun.

Can you draw my pretty leaves?

See the bud at the end of my stem.

Watch for the leaves that are in that bud.

It will open soon.

Can you make it open?

10

stem	reach	toward	that
up end	bud	open	

[32]

LESSON TWENTY-NINE.

The Bean's Story. V.

bean vine
What do you think of me now?

I have grown big and tall.

Here are two little bean pods.

You see the tiny beans in the pod.

Here are some white flowers.

They will soon fall off.

Watch for more bean pods.

By and by the tiny beans will grow big.

What will they look like?

My work will soon be done.

[33]

Think what I have done for you.

You may thank Him who gave me life.

LESSON THIRTY.

Cursive: We planted a bean. It looked like [drawing] One day it looked [drawing] like this. By and by it had leaves. Then it looked [drawing] like this. Mary.

[34]

LESSON THIRTY-ONE.

The Lily.

lilylily
Look at this pure white lily.

Jesus wants us to think how the lilies grow.

He said, "Consider the lilies of the field, how they grow."

Who made the beautiful white dress for this lily?

If God cares for the lily, will He not care for us?

He wants us to obey Him as the lily does.

Then He will clothe us as He does the lily.

He will make our lives pure and beautiful.

11

LESSON THIRTY-TWO.

still life fruit
Here are grapes, an apple, and bananas.

Which do you like best?

Can you tell where bananas grow?

Do not be afraid to eat plenty of good, ripe fruit.

All who obey God shall eat fruit from the tree of life in the earth made new.

LESSON THIRTY-THREE.

A Friend of Ours.

Yes, the sheep is a friend.

Your warm dress was made from her coat. She gives it away in the spring. In the fall you are glad to put it on.

The sheep are timid.

sheep
They need some one to care for them.

The man who cares for the sheep is the shepherd.

The little sheep are lambs.

Jesus calls us His lambs.

So you can say, "The Lord is my shepherd, I shall not want."

A good shepherd would give his life for his sheep.

lilylilylilylily
Jesus gave His life for us.

King David was a shepherd. One time a lion was going to kill one of his lambs. David killed the lion.

Some day the lion and the lamb shall live together. Yes, and a little child shall lead them.

LESSON THIRTY-FOUR.

milk maids and cows
See how that girl carries the milk.

Look at the girl who is milking.

I never saw any one milk from that side of the cow.

I do not think those girls live in this country.

This must be a milking scene in some country far across the water.

They have some strange ways of doing things in those countries.

[39]

LESSON THIRTY-FIVE.

Pansies
I need not tell you our name.

The children say we look like faces.

Did you ever see any of us look cross?

We are always smiling and happy.

Give us the right kind of food and our size will please you.

cursive: Think of our smiling faces when things do not please you.
[40]

LESSON THIRTY-SIX.

The Lion.

Here is the lion.

Is he not fine looking?

Other beasts are afraid of him.

He is called the king of beasts.

A lamb is not safe with him now.

By and by GOD will make all things new. Then the lion will eat straw like the ox.

[41]

The Bible says that the wolf and the lamb, the lion and the calf, shall lie down together.

Then other beasts will not be afraid of the lion.

Then you can pet the lion as you do your cat now.

cats Here are some cousins of the lion.
Do you want to live in that home?

Only the pure in heart shall live in the earth when it is made new.

[42]

LESSON THIRTY-SEVEN.

rabbits
These little bunnies are having a fine time.

They know good food when they find it.

13

Do you know what kind of food bunnies like best?

Look at their eyes. Are they like kitty's eyes?

[43]

LESSON THIRTY-EIGHT.

country lane
I think this must be the home of our bunnies.

Does it look like the country homes you have seen?

Look at the road and the trees.

Are the trees alike?

Do you think it would have been nice if God had made all trees alike?

[44]

LESSON THIRTY-NINE.

Wheat and Tares.

wheat
Do you know what is made from wheat? If you do not, ask some one to tell you.

When Jesus was on earth, He talked about wheat. At the same time He talked about some bad plants, called tares.

He said that a man sowed some good seed in a field. Then some one came and sowed tares in the same field. The good seed was wheat.

So the wheat and tares were growing in the same field.

The servant wanted to root up the tares. The man said, "No; let them grow together until the harvest."

[45]

weed
Why did Jesus tell this story? See what He says about it:—

"'The field is the world. The good seed are the children of the kingdom. But the tares are the children of the wicked one. The harvest is the end of the world. The reapers are the angels."

The harvest is very near.

That is when Jesus comes in the clouds of heaven.

The reapers will take the children of the kingdom home to heaven.

The children of the wicked one will be destroyed.

Are we wheat or tares?

[46]

LESSON FORTY.

flock of sheep and shepherd
Here is a shepherd with his flock.

14

I think he must be a kind shepherd.

See how tenderly he carries the little lamb.

Jesus is our Shepherd. Isaiah says of Him, "He shall gather the lambs with His arms."

So He will tenderly care for all His lambs now.

Soon He will come to take them to the home He is preparing.

[47]

LESSON FORTY-ONE.

rowboats at sea wreck in background
Will they reach the shore?

I wonder what they think?

Once Jesus was with His disciples on the lake.

There came a great storm. Jesus was asleep.

The disciples worked like these men are working.

At last they called to Jesus.

When He awoke He spoke to the wind, and there was a calm.

[48]

LESSON FORTY-TWO.

Washing Dishes.

girls washing dishes
"Good morning, Mary! How can you sing while washing dishes? I always feel cross, for I do not like to wash dishes."

"Well," said Mary, "I must tell you my secret. I used to feel cross, too. Now I think about the lesson I am to learn while washing dishes. Jesus said that we should make the inside of the cup clean as well as the outside."

[49]

"Oh, yes, mama tells me to wash the dishes clean, but I get so tired of them."

"But, Nellie, you do not see the lesson we are to learn. You know we try to look very pretty when people see us. We want them to think that we are pure and clean. When I am washing dishes, I think how Jesus makes my heart pure and clean. He says, Though your sins be red, I will make them white as snow."

Nellie went home happy. Do you think she can sing now while washing dishes?

bee hive, lion, flower
Drawing Lesson.
[50]

LESSON FORTY-THREE.

Creation. I.

"In the beginning God made the heaven and the earth."

15

The earth did not look as it does now. Every thing was very beautiful.

Green grass covered all the valleys, hills, and mountains.

There were lovely lakes and rivers.

The air and water were clear and pure.

There were no swamps nor deserts, and there were no weeds. The most beautiful flowers were seen in every place.

We cannot think how lovely every thing was at that time. The earth was full of the love of God.

"And God saw every thing that He had made, and it was very good."

[51]

LESSON FORTY-FOUR.

Creation. II.

God did not make the earth as man makes things.

"He spake, and it was done." He was six days in making the heaven and the earth.

"And God said, Let there be light, and there was light."

This was on the first day.

The second day He made the air.

At this time water covered all the earth.

The third day He made the dry land appear. He called the dry land earth.

Then the rivers, lakes and seas were made.

He spake, and all the earth was covered with green grass.

[52]

Then came the herbs and trees.

The herbs were bearing seed.

The trees were bearing fruit.

The seed and fruit were to be food for man.

LESSON FORTY-FIVE.

Creation. III.

On the fourth day He said, "Let there be lights in the heaven."

The sun, moon, and stars were to give light upon the earth.

He made the sun to rule the day.

He made the moon to rule the night.

Now there was light; there was air, there was water.

But there were no birds in the air.

There were no fishes in the water.

[53]

On the fifth day He made all the birds and fishes.

Now there were animals in the air.

There were animals in the water.

But there were no animals on the land.

On the sixth day God made all the land animals.

The same day He said, "Let us make man in our image."

He gave them the seed of the herbs and the fruit of the trees for food.

"And God saw every thing that He had made, and it was very good."

Thus the heavens and the earth were made.

[54]

LESSON FORTY-SIX.

Creation. IV.

On the seventh day God rested from all His work.

He blessed it and made it holy.

He calls the Sabbath His holy day.

On the seventh day He looked at the things He had made and called them very good.

On the Sabbath we should stop our work and our play. God wants us to be happy on that day.

It makes us happy to look at the lovely things He has made for us.

He wants us to remember Him and thank Him for His love.

He told us to remember the Sabbath day to keep it holy.

[55]

LESSON FORTY-SEVEN.

Creation. V.

God loved Adam and Eve. He wanted them to be very happy. So He gave them every thing that was good for them.

He planted a garden in Eden. That was their home. We have never seen such a lovely home as that was. But if we live in the earth made new, we shall see the Garden of Eden. In that garden was "every tree that was good for food," and pretty to look at. All the fruit was perfect.

Then there was the river to water the garden. By the river was the tree of life.

The Lord put Adam into the garden to care for it. So there was a happy family in a lovely home.

[56]

landscape
"Thus the heavens and the earth were finished, and all the host of them." Genesis 2:1.
[57]

Lucifer son of the morning
SATAN was once a beautiful, powerful angel in Heaven. His name then was Lucifer, which means, "Son of the Morning," or, "Shining One, Son of the Dawn." His position in Heaven, his beauty, power, and final end, are well described in Ezekiel 28:12-19.

Lucifer, or Satan, is, next to God and Christ, the wisest being in the universe, for God said, "Thou sealest up the sum, full of wisdom." Verse 12.

He was a very beautiful being, for the text says he was "perfect in beauty." Verse 12.

He has been in the Eden home of Adam and Eve. "Thou hast been in the garden of God." Verse 13.

He was a great musician, and doubtless led the music and singing of the hosts of angels in their morning and evening songs of praise to God. Verse 13 says, "The workmanship[58] of thy tabrets and of thy pipes was prepared in thee in the day that thou wast created."

Satan as an angel
Lucifer after the Fall.
"Prince of the power of the air."
The above text shows that he was "created" by the power of God. All the angels were created full grown, and not born as children. Hence this text is describing some heavenly being.

"Thou art the anointed cherub that covereth; and I have set thee so." Verse 14. Lucifer's position was by the throne of God, with his wings outstretched above it.

The ark built by Moses was a type of heavenly things. On the top of this ark were two cherubim with their wings covering the ark where the glory of God rested. See Exodus 25:20. This represents Lucifer's position as covering cherub, close to the throne of God in heaven.

Lucifer was "the anointed cherub." Anciently the prophets of the Lord anointed the kings to show that they were appointed of God to govern and command. Lucifer was, next to the Son of God, the anointed commander of the hosts of heavenly angels.

All his wisdom, beauty, power, and position were given him by God who had created him. The Creator fitted him for the work He wished him to do, and the place He desired him to occupy. Lucifer owed everything which he possessed to his Lord.

But, like some people who have riches and power, he become proud of his glory. He forgot that it was all the gift of God. The text says, "Thine heart was lifted up because of thy beauty." Eze. 28:17.

The Son of God was above him, and equal with His Father. Lucifer was second to Christ; but, considering his beauty and power, he decided that he ought to be equal with God.

The prophet Isaiah says of him, "Thou hast said in thine[59] heart, I will exalt my throne above the stars of God: I will be like the Most High." Chapter 14:13, 14.

But Jehovah could not permit this. The very thought of it by Lucifer was sin, for it was pride and the exaltation of self. Only the Son of God could be equal with the Father.

Then rebellion came into the heart of Lucifer. He went among the angels and told his story. They loved him as their leader, and many took sides with him.

18

The loyalty of all the angels was tested. Nearly one-half their number took sides with Lucifer. Then there was open rebellion in Heaven. Lucifer had a vast army at his command, and he felt strong enough to defy God.

But rebellion could not be allowed in Heaven. The rebel host must be disposed of in some way. God could destroy them at once, for if He could create them He could also destroy them.

But Lucifer had charged God with being partial and severe, and claimed that the laws of Jehovah were not needed in Heaven. So God allowed the rebellion to develop and do its work, that all the universe might see the awful results of sin, and the final fate of sinners. This will be an object lesson through all eternity.

Note.—The twenty-eighth chapter of Ezekiel tells of the overthrow of the prince of Tyrus, or the city of Tyre, which was a very strong, wealthy, proud, and wicked city on the Mediterranean Sea, near Palestine.

But by reading verses 12-15, it will be seen that this chapter has a double application, and that these verses refer more especially to some being standing at one time in a high position in heaven. It shows him to have been very wise, beautiful, and powerful, and near the presence of the Almighty God.

Such a description can apply only to Lucifer, now known as the devil, and Satan, described in the accompanying lesson. The Bible is full of object lessons; and kingdoms, men, and events are often taken to teach important lessons. Christ did much of His teaching by parables. He took things as He found them in the world to illustrate and make forcible great Gospel truths.

In this chapter the power and beauty, the pride and wickedness, and the final overthrow of Tyre were taken to represent the high position of Lucifer in heaven, his sin of pride and rebellion, and his final fall.

[60]

Angels and Satan falling from heaven
"I beheld Satan as lightning fall from Heaven."
[61]

Satan Marshaling His Host.Satan Marshaling His Host.Satan Marshaling His Host.Satan Marshaling His Host.
LUCIFER and his angels had become God's enemies, or rebels against His government. They could not be allowed to remain in Heaven.

The Son was appointed by the Father to take command of the true angels, and drive out the rebel host. Lucifer took command of the angels who had rebelled with him, and was determined to hold his place in Heaven.

Then "there was war in heaven: Michael [Christ] and His angels fought against the dragon; and the dragon fought and his angels." Revelation 12:7.

When Lucifer sinned and fell, his character and work were so changed that the beautiful name he had in Heaven was also changed. In Revelation 12:9, he is called "the dragon," "that old serpent," "the devil," and "Satan."

Of course Satan could not win in such a warfare. "He was cast out into the earth, and his angels were cast out with him." Revelation 12:9.

In Isaiah 14:12, we read, "How art thou fallen from Heaven, O Lucifer, Son of the Morning! how art thou cut down to the ground."

Christ refers to this when He said to His disciples, "I beheld Satan as lightning fall from Heaven." Luke 10:18.

When Satan knew that he had lost Heaven forever, his[62] heart was filled with anger and hatred for all that was good. His history since then shows that from that time his motto was, "Evil, be thou my good."

Lucifer with back of hand on forehead
"How art thou fallen, O Lucifer, Son of the Morning."

19

Revenge filled his heart in which the love of God once abode, and all his wonderful powers were turned against God and His work. Every artful device of evil angels has been used since then to lead men to follow them in sin and rebellion against God.

It is well for man to know the strength of the foe he has to meet. Satan and his angels have on earth the same wisdom which they had in Heaven before their fall. To this is added six thousand years of experience in their awful work.

In Heaven Satan's influence was so great that he was able to deceive and lead into rebellion nearly half the angels. His power to deceive man is very great.

With such power and influence at his command, we can never overcome the devil in our own strength. When we let go our hold upon God we go onto the enemy's ground, and are "taken captive by him at his will." 2 Timothy 2:26.

[63]

But Christ has twice conquered this foe,—once in the great battle in heaven when Satan was cast out, and again as a man on earth when He met all his temptations and came off victorious.

Hence Satan is to Christ a conquered foe. If we trust our Lord fully He will give us strength in every hour of need, and thus we may become "more than conquerors through Him that loved us." Romans 8:37.

Paul calls Satan "The prince of the power of the air." Ephesians 2:2. He it is who causes the terrible cyclones, the tidal waves, and other awful disasters. Only the restraining hand of God prevents him from bringing destruction to the world more awful than it has yet known.

In Hebrews 2:14, we learn that the devil has "the power of death." This is so because sin brought death, and Satan is the author of sin. He claims all who die as his. Only the power of God can bring them from "the land of the enemy" at the resurrection.

But some glad day sin and death and Satan will be destroyed. Paul declared that Christ, by His death, opened the way by which He "might destroy him that had the power of death, that is, the devil." Hebrews 2:14.

The Lord says through the prophet Ezekiel, "I will bring forth a fire from the midst of thee, it shall devour thee, and I will bring thee to ashes. . . . Thou shalt be a terror, and never shalt thou be any more." Ezekiel 28:18, 19.

Then, with the stain of sin entirely removed, God will have a clean universe, as free from sin as it was before rebellion entered heaven.

[64]

Landscape
The Dominion of All Created Things Was Given to Man.
[65]

The First Dominion.In
IN six days the Creator formed the earth and fitted it up as the home of mankind. When finished it was very beautiful with trees, flowers, and fruits.

Before man was created, God also made the birds, fishes, and all the dumb animals and creeping things. The world was then ready for its master,—man.

"And God said, Let us make man in Our image, after Our likeness. . . . So God created man in His own image." Genesis 1:26, 27.

Man was the last and most perfect work of the great creation week. He was in the "image of God." He looked like his Creator.

Some, at least, of the wisdom of God was given to him. He could talk, and think, and reason. As we study God's Word, and learn about Him, He helps us and teaches us. Thus we grow more like Him, and He gives us more of His wisdom.

After creating man, God made for him a beautiful garden which was to be the home of Adam and Eve. This was a sample of what their children were to make of the rest of the world.

This home was called the "Garden of Eden." It was very beautiful, for "out of the ground made the Lord God to grow every tree that is pleasant to the sight, and good for food." Genesis 2:9.

[66]

"God said, Behold, I have given you every herb bearing seed, which is upon the face of all the earth, and every tree, in which is the fruit of a tree yielding seed." This shows what is the best kind of food for man to eat. "And to every beast of the earth, and to every fowl of the air, and to every thing that creepeth upon the earth, wherein there is life, I have given every green herb for meat." Genesis 1:29, 30. This was a perfect diet. The Lord did not intend that His creatures should be killed and eaten for food.

A beautiful "river went out of Eden to water the garden." The tree of life was also there. This tree had wonderful power. It would preserve life, and so long as one should eat of it he would never die.

statement not backed up by the Bible
"Heavenly visitors taught them about God."
"And the Lord God took the man, and put him into the garden of Eden to dress it and to keep it." Genesis 2: 15. Man was not to live in idleness, but must care for the beautiful home which God had prepared for him.

After all was completed the Lord gave to man the earth and all that was in it. David said, "The earth hath He given to the children of men." Psalms 115:16.

Man was also to be ruler of all that was on the earth.[67] For the Lord said, "Be fruitful, and multiply, and replenish the earth, and subdue it; and have dominion over the fish of the sea, and over the fowl of the air, and over every living thing that moveth upon the earth." Genesis 1:28.

Even the beasts loved man and delighted to obey him. There was no fear in that wonderful home. All was love, and happiness, and peace.

Christ and the beautiful angels from Heaven often visited the happy pair in Eden.

These heavenly visitors taught them about God and His love, and gave them such instruction as would help them to take proper care of their earthly home.

Before Satan could reach them with his temptations, angels were sent from Heaven to warn them of his fall, and of his desire to bring ruin upon then, as he had already done upon the angels who sinned with him. In this the loving, tender care of God for His creatures was manifested.

garden with angel in armor entering
Satan Entering Eden.
God is love. He did not wish sin to enter the world; yet He made man free so that he could choose wrong doing if he preferred it to God's way, after knowing of the dreadful results of sin.

[68]

The Dominion Lost.The Dominion Lost.The Dominion Lost.The Dominion Lost.
THE love and obedience of every intelligent being must be tested. Tests make character. If we obey God's laws and walk in His ways, we become in character like God and sinless angels.

We must have a good character before we are fit to enjoy the beautiful home Christ is preparing for those who are faithful. God will give us a good character, and help us to obey, if we ask Him.

If we refuse to let God help us do right, we are out of harmony, or at war with Him and Heaven. We then come into harmony, or union, with Satan and his angels, and when sin is destroyed we must perish with it.

Sin makes people unhappy, and God hates it because He loves everybody. Happiness can be found only in obedience, or doing right.

Before sin reached Eden, Adam and Eve knew nothing of evil. So their only test was in regard to one special tree planted in the garden. It was called the "tree of knowledge of good and evil."

God said of the fruit of this tree, "Ye shall not eat of it, neither shall ye touch it, lest ye die." Genesis 3:3. If they kept away from this tree they would never know evil. At that tree was the only place where Satan could meet them to tempt them.

One day the curiosity of Eve led her to come near the[69] forbidden tree. By so doing she placed herself where Satan could tempt her, and he was there to meet her as he always meets us when we go in the way of temptation.

Satan did not come in his own form, but in the shape of a beautiful Serpent. Eve would have known him in his real person, for angels had told the first pair about the rebellion of Satan and his angels. Satan never comes to us as he really is. He comes as a deceiver, just as he came to Eve in the garden.

The serpent told Eve that the forbidden fruit was good, and began to eat some of it. Probably he told her that it gave him power to talk. Eve looked at it and thought about it. The more she looked at it the more she wanted some of it.

But she told the serpent that the Lord had forbidden them to eat of it, for if they did they should "surely die."

Another bit of story not backed by the Bible
Angels sent to tell the first pair about the rebellion of Satan and his angel.
But the serpent said, "Ye shall not surely die." "See, I am eating of it and it does me no harm. In fact, I feel better all the time I am eating of this fruit."

"For God doth know that in the day ye eat thereof, then your eyes shall be opened, and ye shall be as gods, knowing good and evil." Genesis 3:5.

The devil's statement was partly true and partly a lie. And in all his work he will mix enough truth with his lies to deceive those who do not know him and his ways well enough to see the difference.

[70]

It is true that the fruit of that tree would make those wise who ate of it. It would make them wise in the knowledge of evil, and the Lord did not want them to know anything of evil. Such knowledge brings death.

But Satan lied when he said, "Ye shall not surely die," and he knew it. He has been telling this lie ever since. The Lord has said, "The soul that sinneth it shall die."

Eve believed the devil instead of God. She ate of the fruit and gave to Adam, and he ate of it.

The first result of their sin was shame. They saw that they were naked. Then they made themselves aprons of fig leaves, and hid themselves so that none should see them. Sin always brings shame.

But they could not hide from God. He called them and asked what they had been doing.

Adam and Eve trying to avoid God
Hiding from God.
Then they began to make excuses and to blame others, just as we often do when it is found out that we have done wrong; but they could not deceive their Creator. He told them they should have a life of toil and trouble, and would finally die. Then they were driven from their beautiful garden home.

After that the earth was to be the battle ground between good and evil, between Satan and the Gospel. The Garden of[71] Eden contained so many of the beautiful things of God that it was too sacred to become such a battle ground. Sin must not mar it. So man was driven from it to build for himself, as best he could, a new home which he must keep in order by hard work.

22

The earth was cursed with weeds and thistles; but this was not a real evil to fallen man; for while sin is in the world even hard work is a blessing because it helps to keep people out of mischief. It has been truly said that Satan always finds work for idle hands to do.

By disobeying God and obeying Satan man became the servant of sin and Satan. Paul says, "Know ye not, that to whom ye yield yourselves servants to obey, his servants ye are to whom ye obey?" Romans 6:16.

angel pointing out
Driven from Eden.
By obeying Satan man lost his dominion of the earth, and it passed into the hands of Satan. Thus he became "the god of this world."

[72]

Adam and Eve mourning
"To them, bowed low with grief for sin, the shining ones made known the way to heaven."
[73]

The Promised Redeemer.The Promised Redeemer.The Promised Redeemer.The Promised Redeemer.The Promised Redeemer.
WHEN one person is owned by another person, and has to work for him, he is called a slave, or a bond-servant, because he is in bondage, and not free to do what would be best for himself.

So it is with one who lets himself be controlled by the evil instead of by the good. The word devil is like the word evil, and means the same. To do evil is to do as the devil wishes us to do. Put d before evil, and you will see where evil comes from.

A slave can not get free from a cruel master. He has no money to buy his own freedom, and no power to get away. If he tries to escape, he is followed and caught, and brought back again to work for his hateful owner.

Adam and Eve really sold themselves to Satan—the evil, the devil—by doing as he wanted them to do. They traded their happiness for the knowledge of wrong which he promised them, and which he gave them.

Thus he became their owner, or master, instead of God who had made them, and to whom they really belonged.

Now they could not get free, and as the wages, or end of sin, is death, they must serve Satan all their lives and then die, without any hope of another life beyond this one.

God and Christ and the angels all pitied man in this sad condition, and Christ offered to leave Heaven and come to this earth and give His life for man's life.

[74]

Only in this way could He buy back, or redeem man (meaning everybody), so that all who want to be free from the service of Satan and sin can escape death, which is "the wages of sin."

Sometimes a rich man buys a slave from his cruel master, so that the poor man can be free and happy. So Jesus did for us.

We get free from Satan by thanking God for this plan to save us, and asking Him, for Christ's sake, to forgive our sins and help us to live a good life, away from our old master, the evil.

This is what the word Redemption means. It is buying back something that has been sold into bondage. Jesus bought us back after we had sold ourselves to Satan.

"Ye are not your own, for ye are bought with a price," "the precious blood [the life] of Christ." 1 Corinthians 6:19, 20; 1 Peter 1:18, 19.

This "good news," or Gospel of Salvation, was told to Adam and Eve as well as to the shepherds on the plains of Bethlehem hundreds of years afterward, so that all could have a chance to obey God by being made free from the power of Satan.

Adam and Eve desolate
"They traded their happiness for the knowledge of wrong."
[75]

The First Brothers.The First Brothers.The First Brothers.
CAIN and Abel were the first brothers who ever lived on the earth. Cain, the elder brother, was a farmer. Abel was a shepherd, and cared for his father's sheep.

The Bible does not tell us about them when they were boys, but when they were grown it says they both brought offerings to the Lord. Abel brought a lamb as his offering, but Cain brought the fruits of the ground.

The Lord had told them to bring a lamb for an offering, because it would cause them to think of Christ, for He was "the Lamb of God" who was to die for the sins of the world.

The offerings of Cain and AbelThe offerings of Cain and Abel
Before Jesus came to die, men showed their faith in Him by bringing a lamb for their sins. God accepted the offerings of all who were sorry for their sins, and forgave them. This was the Gospel in the Old Testament. Christ was the "Lamb slain from the beginning of the world," because, before the world began the plan was laid that He should die for man if he sinned.

Abel had faith in God. His heart was filled with love because a way had been made by which sinners could return to God, receive pardon, and finally be taken to a new Eden home.

Abel brought a lamb from his flock, and offered it to God for his sins. Looking at the lamb of his sacrifice he saw Christ, the dying Lamb, on the mountain of Calvary. His faith was "counted to him for righteousness," meaning that[76] God called him good. His sins were forgiven. God was pleased with the offering brought by Abel, and so He sent down fire from heaven and burned up the sacrifice; but not so with Cain's fruit.

Then the heart of Cain was like the heart of Satan,—filled with hatred and rebellion against God. He could see the beautiful Garden of Eden which had been the home of his parents, but he could not enter it. An angel with a flaming sword guarded the gateway.

The next act was to kill his brotherThe next act was to kill his brother
In his heart he charged God with cruelty in shutting them out of the garden, and dooming mankind to a life of labor and sorrow. He did not accept with gratitude the wonderful sacrifice made by the Son of God to redeem the world.

He preferred to talk of what he called the cruelty of the Creator in punishing the race. Instead of offering in sacrifice a lamb, which only could represent[77] the sacrifice of Christ, he brought the fruits of the ground. He thought as sometimes people do now, that what we have to offer is good enough, even if it is not just what the Lord calls for.

In Cain's offering there was nothing to point to the offering of Christ. There was no blood showing that death follows sin, and that Christ was to bear it for us. It was in every way contrary to God's plan, and so it showed no faith. There was therefore no Gospel in it, and no salvation. The Lord did not accept Cain's offering, and there was no answering fire.

As Cain saw the difference, he charged God with partiality, and then began to hate his brother, as all wicked people hate the good. The next act was to kill his brother, which was the result of his hatred.

Then the Lord spoke to Cain and asked him, "Where is thy brother Abel?" Cain tried to cover up his sin by lying about it, as some people try to get out of trouble now. He said, "I know not; Am I my brother's keeper?"

But the Lord knew all about it, for Cain could not hide his sin from the Lord any more than we can hide ours. The Lord sent him forth as a wanderer in the earth, and a hateful look marked his face as long as he lived. Faces show character.

[78]

people perishing in flood
Outside the Ark
[79]

Destroyed by a Flood.Destroyed by a Flood.Destroyed by a Flood.Destroyed by a Flood.

BEFORE the flood men lived to be nearly a thousand years old. They were much larger and stronger than they are now. Living so long they became very wise and very rich.

For many years there were those who believed in God and obeyed Him. But in time most of the people forgot Him and became very wicked.

"And God saw that the wickedness of man was great in the earth, and that every imagination of the thoughts of his heart was only evil continually. . . . And the earth was filled with violence." Genesis 6:5, 11.

So the Lord said He would bring a flood of waters on the earth to drown all the wicked people.

But Noah and his family were faithful to God. So He told Noah to build a great boat, called the ark. It was so large that it would hold all his family, and some of all kinds of animals and birds. It also had room to hold food for them for many days.

The world was warned in regard to the flood, for Noah was one hundred and twenty years building the ark. Part of this time he preached, telling the people of the coming flood, and part of the time he worked on the ark.

Ark and animals in pairs
Entering the Ark.

But the people were too busy and too wicked to heed the preaching of Noah. They only laughed at him for wasting[80] [81] his time and money building such a great boat so far from water deep enough to float it.

When the ark was finished, the Lord caused the animals from the forest, and the birds of the air, to come to it. They came two and two, and went to their places in perfect order. The angels of the Lord were leading them, although none could see them. It must have been a wonderful sight.

When all were in the ark, the Lord shut the heavy door. Then the rain came down and the thunder rolled. The crust of the earth was broken up, and the water under the surface was thrown up in great water-spouts.

The water rose higher and higher. It rained forty days and forty nights. Men and animals climbed to the tops of the highest mountains. But finally these were all covered. Then all the human beings, the birds, and the animals on the whole earth were drowned.

But all that were in the ark rode safely on the waters. The power of God protected the ark through all this terrible time.

Then the Lord caused a wind to blow, which dried up the water. After floating one hundred and fifty days, the ark rested upon the top of Mount Ararat.

After this Noah waited forty days, and then he opened the window in the top of the ark and sent out a raven and a dove. But they found no place to rest, and so returned to the ark.

Seven days after, he sent out another dove, and in the evening it returned with an olive leaf in its mouth. After another seven days, he again sent out a dove, but it did not return.

Finally the water was fully dried up, and God told Noah that he and all the birds and animals could leave the ark. They must have been very glad to be on the land once more, for they had been in the ark a year and seventeen days.

[82]

25

Noah was very thankful to God for saving their lives. "And Noah builded an altar unto the Lord, and took of every clean beast, and of every clean fowl, and offered burnt offerings on the altar." Genesis 8:20.

Noah's Sacrifice.Noah's Sacrifice.Noah's Sacrifice.Noah's Sacrifice.Noah's Sacrifice.Noah's Sacrifice.Noah's Sacrifice.

The Lord was pleased with this offering, for it showed that Noah was still true to God, and had faith in Jesus Christ, the great Sacrifice for the sins of the world.

Then the Lord said that He would not again destroy the earth with a flood. And as a covenant, or pledge in regard to this promise, He set the beautiful rainbow in the clouds.

As all the wicked were destroyed from the earth, the Lord made a new start with the family of faithful Noah, to raise up a people that would obey Him and be finally redeemed, or brought back to the first dominion.

Jesus said, "As the days of Noah were, so shall also the coming of the Son of man be. For as in the days that were before the flood they were eating and drinking, marrying and giving in marriage, until the day that Noah entered into the ark, and knew not until the flood came and took them all away; so shall also the coming of the Son of man be." Matthew 24:37-39.

[83]

The Tower of Babel.The Tower of Babel.The Tower of Babel.

NOT long after the flood, some of the descendants of Noah forgot God who had saved their fathers in the ark. They began to worship idols as the people did before the flood.

Then Nimrod gathered these wicked people together and went with them to the plain of Shinar. Nimrod was a grandson of Ham, and a great grandson of Noah. He was a mighty hunter, and became famous in the earth.

The Lord wanted the people to move in small companies into different places all over the earth. In this way it could be best settled and subdued, or cultivated.

Nimrod wanted to build large cities and keep the people together. In this way he wished to establish a government that would finally rule the world.

"The beginning of his kingdom was Babel." In this city they decided to build a great tower that would be the wonder of the world. They thought they would make the tower so high that they could go to the top of it and be safe if ever there came another flood.

God had promised that He would never again destroy the world by a flood, but these people did not believe God. They forgot that if God could bring a flood on the earth He could also destroy any city and tower that man could build.

For a long time the work of building this great tower went forward rapidly. It was finished inside into many rooms, some of which were used as temples for idol worship.

[84]

Then the people were scattered abroad in the earth.Then the people were scattered abroad in the earth.

How long they were at work on this tower we do not know, but it reached to a great height. The builders were much pleased with their work, and praised the gods of silver and gold. They believed that these idols were giving them success.

Then the Lord interfered with their work. He would teach the people that He was the true and all-powerful God. He would show to the world that their idols could not help them nor give them any real success.

It is always best to trust and obey the true God. He alone can give true happiness and success. Some people now trust in their riches. Some trust in their strength. Some trust in their education. But almost every day we hear of some rich man who has lost his wealth, some strong man who loses his strength by sickness, some educated man who has failed in his work.

[85]

26

But the man who obeys God and walks in His ways in this world, is sure of success. He may not be rich, nor strong, nor have great learning, but he will have true happiness and a reward by and by greater than all the world can give.

Before building the tower of Babel the whole world spoke one language, and the people could understand one another easily. But when their work seemed most successful, the Lord made them speak different languages. None could understand what the others were saying.

Soon all was confusion. If the workmen ordered brick sent to them, they got mortar. If they ordered stone, perhaps they got wood. This made the workman very angry, and their work ended in disappointment and strife.

Then the people were scattered abroad in the earth as God intended they should be. The tower was then called the tower of Babel, which means tower of confusion.

Many years afterward the city of Babylon was built around this tower, and the tower was used as a temple of their god Belus. The tower was then named the Temple of Belus.

[86]

men on camels
"And he went out, not knowing whither he went."
[87]

The Call of Abraham.

The Call of Abraham.The Call of Abraham.The Call of Abraham.The Call of Abraham.
AFTER the people were scattered from Babel, they became more wicked than before. Nearly all turned from the true God, and worshiped idols. Abraham remained true to God; but even his father's household were beginning to worship false gods. The world then was about as wicked as before the flood.

Then God chose Abraham to represent Him in the earth. He would call him the father of the faithful, which means those who have faith, or who believe God. He would give His truth a new start, as He did when He chose Noah before the flood.

God would not destroy the sinners, as He did at the flood, but would call Abraham out from among them. Then through Abraham He would give to the world the knowledge of the only true God.

But the Lord must separate Abraham from his own kindred and friends, and teach him, and fit him to be the father of a nation that should serve Him. Hence Abraham must leave his home, and go where the wicked lives of his friends and relatives would not lead him away from God.

And God said, "Get thee out of thy country, and from thy kindred, and from thy father's house, unto a land that I will show thee." Genesis 12:1.

Abraham obeyed at once. "And he went out, not knowing whither he went." He loved his home, but he loved to[88] obey God more than he loved his home or friends. He did not even know where he was going. He simply trusted God.

The Lord led him to the land of Canaan, or Palestine. Lot, who was his nephew, was the only one of his relatives who went with him.

Abraham was very rich. He had vast flocks and herds and a large number of servants to care for them. Lot had also large flocks and many servants.

When Abraham finally pitched his tents in Canaan, he was distressed to find the country filled with idolatry. Idols were worshiped in the temples and groves, and human beings were sacrificed upon the hills.

But the Lord appeared to him in the night and said, "Unto thy seed will I give this land," and, "I will multiply thy seed as the stars of heaven."

This gave him hope and courage, "And there builded he an altar unto the Lord who appeared unto him." Genesis 12:7. He did the same as Abel and Noah. He offered a lamb. This shows that he believed in Jesus who was to die for the sins of the world.

The Lord prospered Abraham in Canaan, and his wealth, his flocks and herds, increased wonderfully. By the example of his life the Canaanites learned of the true God.

The Departure of Hagar.The Departure of Hagar.The Departure of Hagar.
Wherever he pitched his tent he built an altar to the true God, and morning and evening called his large family together to sacrifice and prayer.

Thus the Canaanites learned of the God of Abraham. They saw that the Lord was with him. But idol worship had so strong a hold upon them that few turned to the true God.

By and by there came a great drought in Canaan. The rain ceased to fall, the streams were dried, and the grass withered. It seemed that his whole encampment must perish.

Then Abraham journeyed to Egypt where he remained[89] until the rains again filled the streams and caused the grass to grow in Canaan.

By this visit to Egypt the people there learned of the true God. Thus, in His own way the knowledge of a promised Saviour was taken by Abraham to the great countries of Canaan and Egypt.

It was God's plan that through Abraham and his descendants the whole world should learn of the "good news" of salvation from sin and death, through Christ who was to suffer for men, and thus buy them back to God and happiness.

But Abraham had no children, and Sarah, his wife, did not believe that God would give her a son. So she got Abraham to marry her Egyptian maid, Hagar. But the Lord said that His promise was not to be fulfilled through Ishmael, the son of this woman, but through a son whom He would give Sarah. So after Isaac was born, Hagar and Ishmael were sent away; for the Lord had said, "In Isaac shall thy seed be called."

[90]

Very dark image with some sparks of fire and brimstone in the background
The Flight from Sodom.
[91]

The Destruction of Sodom.The Destruction of SodomThe Destruction of Sodom.The Destruction of Sodom.The Destruction of Sodom.
ABRAHAM returned from Egypt "very rich in cattle, in silver, and in gold." Lot was still with him, and their flocks and herds became so great that they could not find pasture for them all together.

So Abraham said to Lot, "Is not the whole land before thee? Separate thyself, I pray thee, from me. If thou wilt take the left hand, then I will go to the right; or if thou depart to the right hand, then I will go to the left."

Abraham was the elder, and the choice should have been his. But he was not selfish, and so gave the choice to the younger man, his nephew.

Lot selfishly chose the plain of Jordan. This was the most beautiful and productive portion of all the land of Canaan. And he "pitched his tent toward Sodom."

But Lot did not stop to consider that Sodom and the other cities of the plain were very wicked. He thought only of his own interests, and was soon living in the city of Sodom itself. His daughters married wicked men of Sodom, and so forgot God. Lot could now see the evil of choosing his home among wicked people.

At last Sodom and some of the other cities near it became so wicked that God would not suffer them to remain. He must destroy them from off the earth. But first the Lord would tell Abraham what He was about to do.

28

One day when it was very warm, Abraham sat in the door[92] of his tent. Soon he saw three strangers coming toward him. He ran to them and asked them to come and sit under a tree and rest while he prepared some food for them to eat.

After they had eaten, two of the men went toward Sodom, but the third, who was the Lord, or Christ, remained to tell Abraham that He was about to destroy Sodom.

Then Abraham began to plead for Sodom. He made many requests of the Lord, and finally gained the promise that if ten righteous people could be found in Sodom the city would be saved.

In his child-like faith Abraham felt safe when this promise was made. In the household of Lot alone he thought there must be at least ten who were true to God. But the evil surroundings of Sodom had corrupted even the family of Lot.

The three angelsthe three angelsGenesis 18:1-2
The two angels who left Abraham came to Lot and told him to take his sons and daughters, and flee from the city. But these young persons, who were married to the people of Sodom, would not heed the warning.

Early the next morning the angels told Lot to take his[93] wife and the two daughters who were with him, and hasten out of the city.

But Lot lingered, for he was sorry to know that some of his children, his friends, the beautiful city, and all his wealth must be destroyed. So the angels took hold of them and hastened them out of Sodom.

Then the angel said to them, "Escape for thy life; look not behind thee, neither stay thou in all the plain; escape to the mountain, lest thou be consumed." And then the angel adds, "For I can not do anything till thou be come thither."

The angel had said, "Look not behind thee." But the treasure of Lot's wife was in Sodom. She did not heed the warning of the angel. She loved her beautiful home and the riches of Sodom more than she loved God. She proved unworthy of the deliverance that the angels of God had brought to them, and she turned and looked back to see if God really meant what he said. That very moment she became a pillar of salt, dead and white like a marble statue.

When Lot and his daughters were far away, the Lord rained a horrible tempest of fire and brimstone upon the cities of the plain, and they were utterly destroyed. The very ground where they stood is now covered by the Dead Sea.

Thus God showed His hatred of their awful wickedness. They loved sin, and were not thankful that God had paid the great price of the life of His only Son in order to save them from doing wrong, if they would only ask Him for help to do right. Holding on to sin they perished with it, as many will perish in the last great "lake of fire" "prepared for the devil and his angels." That fire is not being prepared for man; heaven is being fitted up for him. Oh that all would accept it!

Jesus said, "In my Father's house are many mansions; I go to prepare a place for you." Which place are we preparing ourselves for? We are to make the choice.

[94]

Abraham and Isaac.Abraham and Isaac.Abraham and Isaac.Abraham and Isaac.
GOD had promised Abraham that he should be the father of a great nation, and that the land of Canaan should be their home. This was not to come through Ishmael, but through another son.

God had also promised that "in thy seed shall all nations of the earth be blessed." Genesis 22:18. Paul says, in Galatians 3:16, that the "seed" here mentioned is Christ; so Genesis 22:18 is a promise that Christ shall come through the family of Abraham. In Christ all nations of the earth are blessed, although not all of them accept the blessing.

Abraham was called "The friend of God," because he loved and served the Lord so faithfully.

He had a son named Isaac, whom he loved very much. God had told Abraham that Isaac should be his heir, or have all that was Abraham's when he died. All the blessings promised to Abraham were to come to his son Isaac.

But a great trial was to come to Abraham to test his faith in God. The Lord said to him, "Take now thy son, thine only son Isaac, whom thou lovest, and get thee into the land of Moriah; and offer him there for a burnt offering upon one of the mountains which I will tell thee of." Genesis 22:2.

What a terrible test this was! How could God's promise be fulfilled if Isaac should die? But Abraham did not distrust God nor question His command. He believed that if[95] Isaac should die God would "raise him up, even from the dead." Hebrews 11:19.

Early the next morning Abraham took Isaac and two of his servants and prepared for the long journey. They cut the wood and bound it to the back of his beast, and started for the place of sacrifice.

None but Abraham knew of the awful command of God. His heart was very sad as they journeyed three days in silence.

Ascent of Mount Moriah.
On the third day they came in sight of the mountain God had appointed as the place of sacrifice.

"And Abraham said unto his young men, Abide ye here with the ass; and I and the lad will go yonder and worship.

"And Abraham took the wood of the burnt offering, and laid it upon Isaac his son; and he took the fire in his hand, and a knife; and they went both of them together." Genesis 22:5, 6.

As the two walked on in silence, Isaac finally asked, "My father," "behold the fire and the wood; but where is the lamb for a burnt offering?"

This was the first time this question had been asked on[96] the journey. What pain it must have brought to the heart of the loving father! He could not tell him yet, so he said, "God will prepare himself a lamb for a burnt offering."

Abraham not sacrificing Isaac
"Lay not thine hands upon the lad."
At last they came to the appointed place. They built an altar and placed upon it the wood. Abraham must now tell his son the command that God had given. He could keep it no longer.

Isaac heard the message of his fate in sorrow, but he did not resist. Abraham was a hundred and twenty years old, and weak from grief. Isaac was twenty years old, and strong and vigorous. He could have escaped if he had desired to do so, but he, too, had faith in God, and was obedient to his parents.

Isaac let his aged father bind him down to the wood upon the altar, just as Jesus was to let Himself be nailed to a cross of wood. The last good-bye had been said, and the last tender words spoken. Then Abraham raised the knife to slay his son.

But before the stroke could fall, an angel calls to him from Heaven, "Abraham, Abraham!" And the patriarch answers, "Here am I."

[97]

Then the angel said, "Lay not thine hand upon the lad, neither do thou anything unto him; for now I know that thou fearest God, seeing thou hast not withheld thy son, thine only son from me." Genesis 22:12.

What a joyful command! How easy it was to obey it! Then Abraham saw a ram caught in the bushes. This he took and offered upon the altar in the place of his son. Then they journeyed back to their home with joyful hearts. The Lord blessed Abraham still more because he had obeyed Him.

The Lord Directs Abraham's Servant
In Selecting a Wife for Isaac. Genesis 24.

Abraham was willing that Isaac should die, believing it to be best, just as God was willing that Jesus should die for us, knowing it to be best.

Isaac was willing to lay down his own life, just as Jesus was willing to lay down His life for us.

Abraham was spared the awful sorrow of seeing his son die. Another victim was found. But no one could take the place of Jesus. His Father and all the angels in Heaven had to see His dreadful death; and it was all for us.

[98]

Jacob kneeling in front of Isaac
Jacob Deceiving His Father.
[99]

Jacob and Esau.Jacob and Esau.Jacob and Esau.Jacob and Esau.
ISAAC had two sons, named Jacob and Esau. Esau was a little older than Jacob, and was a hunter of wild animals. Jacob was a shepherd, and cared for his father's sheep.

Esau, the daring hunter, was very dear to his father; but Rebekah loved Jacob most because he was so kind and careful.

God had said to Rebekah that "the elder shall serve the younger." So she knew that the Lord would especially bless Jacob, and finally give him the birthright, which meant that he was to have a double portion of his father's wealth, and also become the head of the family when his father died.

The birthright usually went to the eldest son, but the birthright in the family of Isaac must go to the son who would obey God. He was to be the father of God's people,—the children of Israel.

Jacob loved God, and was willing to obey Him. He greatly desired the blessing which the birthright would bring to him. But Esau did not love God nor care to serve Him. He would rather live the wild, free life of a hunter, and do as he chose, than have the birthright.

Jacob did not trust God as he should, for he feared that Esau would have the birthright because he was the eldest son of Isaac. So he studied all the time to find some plan to get it away from Esau.

Angels ascending and descending
Jacob's Dream.
One day Esau had been in the fields hunting, but had found nothing. On the way home he became very hungry. Coming to the tent of his brother he found him preparing his dinner[100] [101] of pottage. "And Esau said to Jacob, Feed me I pray thee, with that same red pottage; for I am faint."

Jacob forgot that he ought to be kind to his brother. He only thought that this was the chance he had been looking for. "And Jacob said, Sell me this day thy birthright."

"And Esau said, Behold, I am at the point to die; and what profit shall this birthright do to me?" So he sold his birthright to his brother for a good dinner.

You see Jacob took a mean advantage of his brother when he was faint and hungry. This made it easier for him afterward to do another great wrong, and deceive his father. One wrong act always makes it easier to do another.

When Isaac was very old he became blind. He was still determined to give the birthright to Esau. So one day he told him to go into the field and kill a deer and make some savory meat, and then he would bless him.

But Rebekah heard it, and she was afraid the Lord would let Esau have the birthright. She thought she must do something to help the Lord keep His promise that Jacob should be head of the family.

So she told Jacob to kill two young goats, and she made savory meat, such as Esau made from venison. Then she dressed Jacob in Esau's clothes, and sent him in to deceive his blind father.

31

This was very wicked, for Jacob told lies to his father to make him think that he was Esau. So through falsehood Jacob got the blessing which made him head of the family.

When Esau returned and learned what Jacob had done, he was very angry. Fearing that his brother would kill him, Jacob fled from his father's house, and went to Mesopotamia, where his mother's family lived.

He felt very sorrowful on his journey. He was afraid that his sin was too great to be forgiven. But one night he confessed[102] it all to God, and then laid his head on a stone for a pillow, and went to sleep.

In the night the Lord gave him a beautiful dream. In it he saw a ladder which reached from earth to heaven. On this ladder there were angels ascending and descending.

At the top of the ladder Jacob saw his Saviour, who told him that He was the God of Abraham and Isaac, and that He would be his God, and make him the father of a great nation. This was because Jacob was sorry for his sins. The Lord promised to go with him on his journey, and finally bring him back again, and that his children should have the land of Canaan for their home.

From this place Jacob journeyed until he came to the home of Laban, his mother's brother. Here he worked hard twenty years.

One night the Lord came to him in a dream, and said, "Arise, get thee out of this land, and return unto the land of thy kindred." Then Jacob prepared immediately to return to Canaan.

Rachel at the well, shepherd in background
Jacob and Rachel.
[103]

Jacob Returns to Canaan.Jacob Returns to Canaan.Jacob Returns to Canaan.Jacob Returns to Canaan.
JACOB had become very rich in sheep and cattle, and had many servants to care for them. His journey back to Canaan was slow. He was very sad because of his sin in deceiving his father.

As he neared his old home he learned that Esau was coming against him with four hundred armed soldiers. Jacob had no soldiers, and was much afraid.

Then Jacob divided his band into two companies, thinking that at least one might escape. He then sent servants with splendid presents to Esau, hoping thus to touch the heart of his brother.

Jacob had now done all that he could do. Then he went by himself to spend the night in prayer. He knew that God could touch the heart of his brother, and this was his only hope.

While praying he suddenly felt a hand laid upon him. He thought it was an enemy seeking his life. He put forth all his strength to escape, but could not. Jacob struggled and wrestled until near morning.

Then the stranger touched him on the hollow of his thigh, and his thigh was put out of joint. Then Jacob knew that he had been struggling with an angel, and not with a man. It was the Lord, his Saviour.

Jacob and Esau hugging amidst large crowd
The Meeting of Jacob and Esau.
Jacob ceased to struggle, and clung to the Angel. He knew he must have divine help or perish. Unless God should work[104]
[105] for him, his brother Esau would overcome and destroy him.

Jacob wrestling with angel
Jacob and the Angel.
But Jacob's faith must be fully tested. The Angel said, "Let me go, for the day breaketh." With the realizing sense of his sins and of his deep need, he clung to his Lord the closer, and cried, "I will not let Thee go, except Thou bless me."

And "he had power over the Angel, and prevailed; he wept and made supplication unto Him; he found Him in Bethel." And the Angel said unto him, "What is thy name? And he said, Jacob. And He said, Thy name shall be called no more Jacob, but Israel [A prince of God]; for as a prince hast thou power with God and with men, and hast prevailed."

32

If we come to God as Jacob did, with confession, with tears, and a perseverance that will not be denied, we can prevail with Him also.

The Lord sent an angel to soften the heart of Esau. At sight of Jacob "Esau ran to meet him, and fell on his neck, and kissed him; and they wept."

Jacob journeyed to the Jordan, which he crossed, and "came in peace to the city of Shechem, which is in the land of Canaan." Here he erected an altar which he named "El-elohe-Israel," which means, "God, the God of Israel."

[106]

Jacob sleeping and dreaming
The Two Dreams of Joseph.
[107]

Joseph in Bondage.Joseph in Bondage.Joseph in Bondage.Joseph in Bondage.Joseph in Bondage.Joseph in Bondage.
JACOB had twelve sons. The ten elder sons were shepherds. They often went far from home to find grass and water for their father's flocks. Joseph and Benjamin, the two younger sons, remained at home with their father.

The elder sons were quarrelsome, and gave their father much trouble. But Joseph was gentle, kind, and truthful. And Jacob "loved Joseph more than all his children." To show his love, Jacob made him a beautiful coat of many colors. These things made his brothers jealous, and they hated him.

But the Lord was pleased with Joseph because he loved to do right and obey his father. God had a great work for Joseph to do. So He gave him two dreams which came true many years afterward.

In his first dream Joseph saw himself and his eleven brothers in the field binding grain into bundles, or sheaves. And his bundle arose and stood upright, and his brothers' bundles bowed down to his bundle.

Probably Joseph did not know what his dream meant. Had he known, he would not have told it to his brothers. When he did tell it to them they hated him more than ever, and said, "Shalt thou indeed rule over us?"

Some time after this Joseph dreamed another dream. In this dream he saw the sun, moon, and eleven stars. And they all bowed down to him. He told this dream to his father and[108] to his brethren. And his father said to him, "Shall I and thy mother and thy brethren indeed come to bow down ourselves to thee to the earth?" But years after, when the famine came, the father, brothers, and their families had to depend on Joseph for even the food which they ate.

Sold to the Ishmaelites.Sold to the Ishmaelites.Sold to the Ishmaelites.Sold to the Ishmaelites.Sold to the Ishmaelites.
One day Jacob sent Joseph to find his brethren, for he wanted to know if they were well. They were many miles away caring for the sheep.

When they saw Joseph coming, these wicked brothers said one to another, "Behold, this dreamer cometh. Let us slay him, and cast him into some pit, and we will say, Some evil beast hath devoured him; and we shall see what will become of his dreams."

But Reuben would not consent to have Joseph killed, so they took off his beautiful coat, and cast him alive into a pit. Soon a company of Ishmaelites came along on their way to Egypt. Then the brothers drew him out of the pit and sold him to be a slave.

[109]

After Joseph was gone, the brothers began to think of their father, and what they should tell him. Then to hide their sin they did another wicked thing. They killed a young goat and put its blood all over Joseph's coat, so it would look as though some wild beast had slain him.

33

Some of the brothers then took the coat to their father, and told him they had found it. They said they had brought it to him to see if it was Joseph's coat.

And Jacob said, "It is Joseph's coat; some evil beast hath devoured him." And Jacob rent his clothes and mourned for his son many days. The wicked brothers deceived their father then, but many years afterward the truth came out, and they had to confess their sin.

And Pharaoh said unto Joseph, Forasmuch as God hath shewed thee all this, there is none so discreet and wise as thou art.And Pharaoh said unto Joseph, Forasmuch as God hath shewed thee all this, there is none so discreet and wise as thou art.

Joseph was sold to a rich man in Egypt, by the name of Potiphar. The Lord blessed Joseph, and Potiphar saw that whatever he did prospered. So he made him steward of all that he had.

But God had a higher place for Joseph, and he must reach it through affliction. In all his troubles it was the Lord who was giving Joseph just the training he needed to fit him for the great work before him.

[110]

Through a wicked and false charge of Potiphar's wife, Joseph was cast into prison. But by his honesty he gained the confidence of the keeper of the prison, and was given charge of the prisoners.

One morning he met the chief butler and the chief baker of the king. They had been cast into prison for some offense, and were looking very sad. He kindly asked the cause, and each said that he had dreamed a strange dream, and could not tell what it meant.

Joseph then said, "Do not interpretations belong to God? tell me them, I pray thee." Then they told their dreams, and the Lord told Joseph their meaning. In three days the butler was to go back to his place with the king, but the baker would be put to death.

Then Joseph told the story of his wrong treatment to the butler, and asked him to tell the king, and try to get him out of prison. But the butler was like many other people who soon forget those who were their friends in trouble. When he got out of prison he forgot all about Joseph and his request.

But God was working all the time in His own way. The king had two dreams in one night, which seemed to mean the same thing. He wanted to understand them, so he called in the wise men of his kingdom, but they could not tell what the dreams meant.

Now get your Bible and read the forty-first and forty-second chapters of the book of Genesis, and see what these dreams were, and how the Lord got Joseph out of prison and made him ruler of Egypt.

When the dreadful famine came, he had corn saved up to keep the Egyptians from starving. Thus the Lord often uses good people to provide for the needs of those who are evil.

But God had another reason for delivering Joseph from prison. What do you think it was?

[111]

Joseph and His Brethren.Joseph and His Brethren.Joseph and His Brethren.Joseph and His Brethren.Joseph and His Brethren.Joseph and His Brethren.

WHEN food began to be scarce with Jacob's family, he sent his ten sons to Egypt to buy corn. Joseph knew his brethren when he saw them, but they did not know him. He did not look like the boy whom they had sold.

As they bowed before him, the ruler of Egypt, he remembered his dreams of many years before. He saw them fulfilled completely. As the sheaves had bowed to his sheaf, so his brethren were now bowing to him.

His heart went out in love for them, but before he should tell them who he was, he wanted to know if they were still wicked, or if their hearts had been changed since he had been separated from them.

Joseph accused them of being spies. But they denied the charge, and said that they were true men, and a family of twelve brethren. Ten were in Egypt, the youngest was with their father, and one was dead. They had never heard of Joseph since they had sold him, and supposed he was dead.

34

But Joseph still accused them of being spies, and shut them all up in prison for three days. These days in prison were days of sorrow. They felt that they were being punished for their cruel treatment of Joseph.

Finally Joseph called them from prison. He told them that all but one could return to their father. He would keep[112] Simeon in prison until they should come back to Egypt, but they must bring their youngest brother when they came, or Joseph would not even see them.

Joseph chose Simeon to remain because he had been the chief actor in their cruelty to him in the past. They returned to their home with heavy hearts.

When the food brought from Egypt was nearly gone, Jacob said to his sons, "Go again, buy us a little food." But they dared not go unless Benjamin should go with them. To this the father at last consented, and they again went to Egypt, taking with them presents for the great governor.

As they started, the sorrowful father raised his hands to heaven and prayed, "God Almighty give you mercy before the man, that he may send away your elder brother, and Benjamin. If I am bereaved of my children, I am bereaved."

When they reached Egypt, their brother Simeon was released, and all were brought to dine at the house of the governor. According to the customs of Egypt, Joseph must eat at a table by himself, and the eleven brothers at a table by themselves. They had been jealous of Joseph in his home, and he wanted to know if they had become better men. So he sent five times as much food to Benjamin. They showed no jealousy now.

But Joseph desired to test them once more. So when the sacks were filled with corn he had his silver drinking cup put secretly into Benjamin's sack.

The eleven brothers departed joyfully, and felt that they had escaped all the perils which they feared. But they had hardly left the city when they were overtaken by the governor's steward.

He said to them, "Wherefore have ye rewarded evil for good?" He then accused them of stealing the cup. They all denied taking it, and felt so sure that they said if it was[113] found with one of them he should die, and all the rest would become servants of the governor.

But the steward would not agree to this. He said, "He with whom it is found shall be my servant; and ye shall be blameless." So all the sacks were opened, and the cup was found in Benjamin's sack.

What will the brothers do now? If still selfish, they will leave their brother to his fate, and go back home. But no, they were changed men. They would now face any peril to save their brother. They rent their clothes to show their grief, and all went back with him to the city, and met the governor.

Then Judah offered to become a slave in the place of Benjamin. This test was enough. Joseph now knew that his brothers were changed.

Joseph on throne with brothers bowing around him
"I am Joseph, your brother."
Did he make slaves of them because they had sold him into bondage when he was a boy?

Find the forty-fifth chapter of Genesis and read what he did, and how the king felt about it when he heard the news, and what became of Joseph's brothers and their father's family.

[114]

Hebrew slaves building
Building the Pyramids
[115]

Moses.Moses.Moses.Moses.
AFTER the death of Joseph "there arose up a new king over Egypt, which knew not Joseph." This king did not wish to remember the good that Joseph had done.

35

The children of Israel had increased in numbers; "and the land was filled with them." The Egyptians feared that if there was a war the Israelites would join their enemies and fight against them.

So the king made them slaves, and set taskmasters over them to make them work. "And they made their lives bitter with hard bondage, in mortar, and in brick, and in all manner of service in the field."

They thought that by their cruelty and the hard work in the fields, they would stop the Israelites from increasing in the land. "But the more they afflicted them, the more they multiplied and grew."

Then the cruel king commanded that all the boys should be killed at their birth. But even this plan did not succeed. The Israelites still increased in the land.

It was at this time that Moses was born. For three months he was carefully hidden at home and cared for by his mother. But she dared not keep him there any longer. So she made an ark of bulrushes, and laying the babe in it, hid it among the flags by the river.

His sister Miriam anxiously watched the little ark while the[116] mother prayed earnestly that her child might not be destroyed. God heard the mother's prayer, for the babe in the little ark was to be used by the Lord to deliver Israel from bondage.

One day the daughter of the king came to the river to bathe. She saw the ark, and sent one of her maids to bring it. When she opened it and saw the beautiful child, she knew why it was there, and said, "This is one of the Hebrews' children." And the child wept, and Pharaoh's daughter pitied it.

Then Miriam came near and said to Pharaoh's daughter, "Shall I go and call to thee a nurse of the Hebrew women, that she may nurse the child for thee? And Pharaoh's daughter said to her, Go. And the maid went and called the child's mother.

"And Pharaoh's daughter said unto her, Take this child away, and nurse it for me, and I will give thee thy wages."

How glad the mother was to again have the care of her own child. He was now safe, for he was the adopted son of Pharaoh's daughter. And better still, he was in the home of his own parents.

The mother had the care of her boy until he was about twelve years old. During these years she taught him carefully about the true God. These lessons he never forgot. They kept him pure and free from the wickedness and idolatry which surrounded him in after years.

From his humble home he was taken to the royal palace, and became the son of Pharaoh's daughter. "And she called his name Moses," which means, drawn out. For, she said, "I drew him out of the water." In his royal home he was trained in all the learning of the Egyptians.

This training fitted him for the highest position in all Egypt. He was the leader in Pharaoh's army, and became a great general. Pharaoh determined that when he died, his daughter's adopted son should be king. But all the plans of[117] man were "overruled by God for the training and education of the future leader of His people." Moses was not to shine as king of Egypt.

One day, when Moses was forty years old, he saw an Egyptian smiting an Israelite. He thought the time had come for him to help his people, so he slew the Egyptian and buried him.

Here Moses made a mistake. He took into his own hands the work which God had promised to do. He supposed his people were to be delivered by warfare, and that he, a skillful general, was to be the leader of the Hebrew armies.

But God had a different plan. By His own hand He would bring His people out of bondage. In the delivering of Israel, He would teach the Egyptians the knowledge of the true God by such wonders and plagues as they could never forget.

maid kneeeling by river to pull Moses' boat out while princess watches
Pharaoh's Daughter finds Moses in the Ark of Bulrushes.

When King Pharaoh learned that Moses had killed the Egyptian, he commanded that he should be slain. But Moses fled toward Arabia, and the Lord led him to Jethro the prince of Midian, whose flocks he cared for during the forty years in which God was preparing him to lead the Israelites out of bondage.

[118]

In Pharaoh's court
Moses and Aaron Before Pharaoh
[119]

The Plagues of Egypt.Moses.Moses.

ONE day as Moses was leading Jethro's flocks near Mount Horeb, he saw a strange sight. A bush was on fire, but it did not burn up. So he went to see what it should mean.

As he came near, a voice from the bush said to him, "Put off thy shoes from off thy feet, for the place whereon thou standest is holy ground." Then Moses knew that it was the Lord who was talking to him from the bush.

The Lord told Moses that the time had come for the Israelites to go free from their bondage in Egypt. He told Moses to start for Egypt, and that his brother Aaron would meet him on the way and go with him.

They were then to go to Pharaoh and tell him that the God of Israel had sent them to him, and that he must let His people go. And he gave Moses wonderful signs to show to Pharaoh, so that he would know that God had sent them.

When Moses and Aaron came before Pharaoh and told him what the Lord had said, he answered, "Who is the Lord that I should let Israel go?" The Hebrew slaves were very valuable to the Egyptians, and they wanted to keep them, and make them do their hard work.

Pharaoh asked them to show a miracle to prove that their God had sent them. Then they performed one of the wonders that the Lord had given to Moses. Aaron cast down his rod,[120] and it became a serpent. Then Pharaoh called in his sorcerers, who were wicked men claiming to have power to do wonderful things. He showed them what Aaron had done with his rod, and asked them if they could turn their rods into serpents.

Then the sorcerers cast down their rods, and they appeared to become serpents also. But while they were looking at them, Aaron's serpent swallowed the serpents of the sorcerers.

But the work of the sorcerers was only a deception of their master, the devil. God only could really give life to the staff of Aaron. Neither the devil nor his servants can give life to anything. But the sorcerers had deceived the people and made their work look like God's work.

By thus deceiving Pharaoh they destroyed the effect of God's miracle, and so the king's heart was hardened against letting Israel go. Satan is ever counterfeiting, or imitating, the work of God. He often makes his lies appear like God's truth. In this way he leads many away from God.

Then God sent ten terrible plagues upon the land of Egypt. Each one was more awful than the one before it. They were sent to teach the Egyptians that the God of Israel was the only true God, and to punish them for refusing to obey Him.

The First Plague.—The River Nile, which they worshiped, was turned to blood.

Second Plague.—An army of frogs, which the Egyptians considered sacred, came up from the river. They went into all the houses, and even into the ovens and the troughs where they made their bread.

Third Plague.—The very dust of Egypt became lice on both man and beast.

Fourth Plague.—Swarms of flies came up until "the land was corrupted" because of them.

Fifth Plague.—A "grievous murrain" came upon the cattle, so that a great many of them died.

[121]

37

Sixth Plague.—Moses sprinkled dust into the air, and it became boils on man and beast.

Seventh Plague.—An awful hail, mingled with fire, smote the land, and killed all men and beasts that were not under shelter.

Eighth Plague.—Clouds of locusts came up and ate every green thing.

Ninth Plague.—"Darkness which might be felt" covered the land for three days. It was so dark that the people did not dare to go out of their houses.

Through nine plagues Pharaoh's heart had remained hard and rebellious against God. Egypt was a ruined country because of this. Now the Lord told Moses that He would send one more plague, more terrible than all the others, and then they would be glad to let His people go.

But before it came, the Hebrews were to "borrow" from the Egyptians "jewels of silver and jewels of gold." For many years they had toiled without wages. What they received at this time was only a partial payment for their long years of service. This silver and gold would be needed when they should build the tabernacle in the wilderness.

Tenth Plague.—At midnight the angel of the Lord was to pass through Egypt and slay the first-born in every house, and the first-born of beasts.

None of the other plagues had come near to the land of Goshen where the children of Israel dwelt. But now they had a part to act or they would suffer with the Egyptians when the destroying angel should pass through the land.

In order to escape, the Israelites must separate from the Egyptians, and come into their own houses. They were to kill a lamb, and, with a bunch of hyssop, strike some of its blood upon the door-posts of their houses. Wherever this was[122] done the destroying angel would "pass over" the house, and all within it were safe.

Pharaoh finds his son
Death of the First-born.
They were also to roast the lamb whole, and eat it at midnight, while the destroying angel was doing his awful work among the Egyptians. They were to eat it standing, their shoes on their feet, their staff in hand, ready for flight.

This most solemn ceremony was called the "passover," because the destroying angel passed over the houses of those who had faith in God's commands and had put the blood upon the door-posts of their houses. The children of Israel were commanded to keep the passover each year as a memorial of their preservation in Egypt.

The passover was also a type of Christ, the Lamb of God. As the blood of the passover lamb upon the door-posts saved those in the house from death, so all will be saved now who confess their sins, believing that the blood of Jesus was shed to save sinners just as surely as the blood of the passover lamb saved those who trusted in it.

[123]

Out of Bondage.Out of Bondage.Out of Bondage.Out of Bondage.Out of Bondage.
"AND it came to pass, that at midnight the Lord smote all the first-born in the land of Egypt; . . . and there was a great cry in Egypt; for there was not a house where there was not one dead."

And Pharaoh "called for Moses and Aaron by night, and said, Rise up, and get you forth from among my people." And he hurried them out of the land of Egypt with their flocks and herds and all they possessed.

When Jacob went into Egypt his whole company numbered only seventy. When Israel left Egypt there were six hundred thousand men, beside women and children. The whole number must have been nearly three millions.

The Lord went before them in a pillar of cloud by day and a pillar of fire by night. And the children of Israel went forward and camped by the Red Sea.

After Israel had left Egypt, Pharaoh became angry because he had let them go. So he took a very large army and pursued after them, and overtook them as they were camped by the Red Sea.

There seemed to be no way of escape for the Israelites. They were hedged in between the mountain and the Red Sea, and behind was the army of Pharaoh. But the Lord had brought them there to test their faith, and show once more how He would deliver them from their enemies.

crossing the sea
The Egyptians Overthrown In the Red Sea.
Moses was commanded to stretch forth his rod, and as he did so the sea parted and left a dry road through which the[124]
[125] Israelites passed over and were safe. And so blind and foolish was Pharaoh that he and his army followed after. When Israel was safe on the other side, Moses again stretched forth his rod, and the sea came back and drowned Pharaoh and all his army.

The Lord cared for his people wonderfully on their journey. At Marah the water was bitter, and they could not drink it. The Lord showed Moses a tree, and told him to cast it into the water; and when he did so it was made sweet and good.

By and by the food which they had brought from Egypt began to fail. The Lord wanted them to learn to trust Him, and so He was willing they should have difficulties to test them. But they did not trust the Lord. They began to complain and find fault with Moses. God had promised to care for them, and if they had only believed Him they would have learned precious lessons and received great blessings.

Then the Lord said to Moses, "I will rain bread from Heaven for you." In the morning they found it on the ground, and called it Manna. Each one gathered just enough to last through the day. This manna would keep fresh and sweet only one day. So they all had to depend on the Lord every day for the food they ate.

In Egypt the people had forgotten the Sabbath. Now the Lord would have them remember it. So on the seventh day no manna was given. But on the sixth day the people gathered enough for two days.

And the Lord kept it sweet for them over the Sabbath. This was a Sabbath lesson for them every week. The Sabbath was made for man, and given to him at creation as a memorial of God's great work of making the world in six days. But Israel had forgotten. God wants His Sabbath kept holy now as well as in the time of Israel in the wilderness.

[126]

people getting water. Some praising God
Water from the Rock.
[127]

When they came to Rephidim there was no water, and the people complained again to Moses. And the Lord told Moses to go to Mount Horeb and smite the rock with his staff. When he did so, water burst from the rock, enough for the whole camp. It was Moses who smote the rock, but the Lord made the waters to flow.

Whenever the camp was pitched after this they found good water flowing from the rock for them. This rock was to make them and us think of Christ, and the water flowing from it represents the living water of the Word of God which He gives to all who want it.

Soon a new danger arose. The Amalekites came out to attack them. Joshua led the armies of Israel against them. While the battle was going on, Moses stood on a hill and raised his hands to God and prayed for the success of Israel. When he became weary and lowered his hands, the Amalekites were successful. Then Aaron and Hur held up the hands of Moses until the sun went down, and Israel gained the victory.

This was to teach Israel that the victory came from God, and that he would hear and answer prayer. It also taught them that they should help their leader, Moses, in the great work he had to do.

[128]

Tabernacle and cloud

39

The Camp and Tabernacle in the Wilderness.
[129]

Mount Sinai.Mount Sinai.Mount Sinai.Mount Sinai.Mount Sinai.

FROM Rephidim Israel journeyed to Mount Sinai. Here God would give His law to the people, and here they were to build the tabernacle for His holy service.

Before this time these people had no books to read. God's Word and His law had been told from father to son, and so remembered. But during the slavery in Egypt this instruction had been forgotten by many, until they had become like the heathen around them.

During their journey God had spoken to Israel only through Moses. But at this time all the people were called together, and God spoke His law to them with His own voice.

The scene which the people saw was terribly grand. There was a thick cloud on the mount, and amidst it were thunderings and lightnings. The whole mountain was shaken with an earthquake.

There was a loud blast of a trumpet from the mount, "so that all the people that was in the camp trembled." Then God spake His law to the people,—the ten commandments recorded in Exodus 20:3-17.

The children of Israel were always to remember this scene. It was to impress upon their minds the greatness and power of God, the importance of His law, and the necessity of obeying it.

Moses was called up into the very presence of God, on the[130] top of the mountain. Here God gave him two tables of stone on which He had written with His finger the same ten commandments that He had spoken in the hearing of all Israel.

God's law is as enduring as the stone on which it was written. These two tables are called "the tables of the covenant." Deuteronomy 9:11. The ten commandments are called God's covenant with His people. "And He wrote upon the tables the words of the covenant, the ten commandments." Exodus 34:28.

David said that His covenant, or law, was "commanded to a thousand generations." Psalms 105:8. It will continue forever. Christ Himself said, "Till heaven and earth pass, one jot or one tittle shall in no wise pass from the law." Matthew 5:17, 18.

Again He said, "Whosoever therefore shall break one of these least commandments, and shall teach men so, he shall be called the least (or, of no account) in the kingdom of heaven." Matthew 5:19.

The Apostle James said, "For whosoever shall keep the whole law, and yet offend in one point, he is guilty of all." James 2:10. Keeping nine of the commandments will not save us. If we break one commandment, the law will condemn us as surely as if we broke all the ten.

Man can not change one single commandment of God's law. If he tries to do so, it is then only a commandment of men. The worship of those who make or keep such commandments is useless, for God will not accept it. Christ said of those who do so, "But in vain do they worship Me, teaching for doctrines the commandments of men." Matthew 15:9.

The only safe course is to take God's law just as He gave it on Sinai, and obey it as He gave it. Of those who will be alive when Christ comes it is written, "Here are they that keep the commandments of God." Revelation 14:12.

[131]

Heaven will be filled with commandment-keeping people; for it is written, "Blessed are they that do His commandments, that they may have right to the tree of life, and may enter in through the gates into the city." Revelation 22:14.

We can not keep these commandments ourselves any more than the children of Israel could in the wilderness. It is for this that Christ died on Calvary. Through Him we can have forgiveness for our sins, and receive help to overcome sin and obey the law of God.

40

While Moses was in the mount God gave him instructions for building the sanctuary. It was to be like the one in heaven. In it the Lord would meet His people and give them such instruction as they needed. Provision was also made in it for sacrifices and offerings, all of which were to show their faith in the Saviour to come.

Moses was in the mountain one-ninth of a year. The faith of the people was not strong enough to endure the long separation from their leader. They did not think he would return to them. They said, "As for this Moses, . . . we wot not what has become of him."

They came to Aaron and said to him, "Up, make us gods, which shall go before us." They would make to themselves a calf as their leader to take the place of Moses, and then go on to the promised land without him. The old habits of idol worship in Egypt had come back to them.

So Israel brought their ornaments of gold to Aaron, and he made of them a golden calf. The calf represented Apis, the god held most sacred by the Egyptians.

The Ark of the Covenant. Ex. 31:18
When it was done the people gathered around it and cried, "These be thy gods, O Israel, which brought thee up out of the land of Egypt." Exodus 32:4.

How could they so soon forget the wonders and plagues brought by the Lord upon Egypt! How could they forget[132] the terrible day when God spake to them His law from the top of Mount Sinai!

And the Lord said to Moses, "Get thee down, for thy people have corrupted themselves." As Moses came in sight of the camp of Israel, and saw their heathen worship, he was filled with horror and anger.

In his hands he bore the tables of the sacred law which they were transgressing. He threw them down, and they were broken in pieces at the foot of the mount. This was to remind the Israelites that they had broken God's law which they had promised to obey. In consequence of this they could not claim the promise He had made them.

Through the pleading of Moses, God spared Israel at this time, but the rebellion and evil must be put away from among them.

Moses called for a separation in the camp. Some had not joined in the idolatry, but through it all had remained true to God. These were asked to take their place at the right hand of Moses. Many others saw how wicked they had been, and repented. These took their stand at the left.

Moses breaking tablets
Moses Breaking the Tables of the Law.
Others were stubborn and would not repent, and would not come by the side of Moses at all. About three thousand of the leaders in wickedness perished at the command of the Lord, and the camp was cleansed.

Aaron confessed his sin in making the golden calf, and[133] was forgiven. The calf was ground to powder and scattered in the waters of the brook from which they drank.

At the command of God, Moses hewed out two more tables of stone, and took them up to Sinai. On these God again wrote His law. When the sanctuary was completed, these tables were placed in a beautiful ark, overlaid with gold. For this reason it was called "The Ark of the Covenant."

This ark was the most sacred thing in all the earthly sanctuary. It was sacred because it contained the tables on which God had written His law. It was deposited in the most holy place, into which none but the high priest ever entered.

On the top of the ark was the mercy seat, and here was where the glory of God rested, and from this place He spake to His people.

When the children of Israel were taken captive by the Babylonians, the ark disappeared, and the Bible makes no mention of it since that time.

[134]

41

The Return of the Spies.

[135]

The Twelve Spies.The Twelve Spies.The Twelve Spies.The Twelve Spies.The Twelve Spies.The Twelve Spies.

AFTER all the work on the tabernacle was done, the Israelites again took up their march toward the promised land. In eleven days they reached Kadesh, near the borders of Canaan.

Here twelve spies—one from each tribe—were sent to view the land. They were gone forty days, and on their return brought samples of the fruit of Canaan. They brought one cluster of grapes, so large that it was carried on a pole between two of the men.

In their report to Moses they said, "We came unto the land whither thou sentest us, and surely it floweth with milk and honey; and this is the fruit of it." Numbers 13:17.

Oh, if they had only been willing to stop there in their report! But they went on to tell that the land was filled with strong nations. There were walled cities that could not be broken down, and there were giants, the sons of Anak.

Then Israel lost all hope and courage, "And all the congregation . . . cried; and the people wept that night." And they murmured against Moses and Aaron, and said, "Would God we had died in Egypt! or . . . in the wilderness. . . . Let us return to Egypt." Numbers 14:2, 4.

Where now was their faith and trust in God? They had forgotten the wonders and plagues and the deliverance from Egypt. They had forgotten the many times God had done[136] wonderful things for them on their journey. Surely a God who could do such things could give them the victory over their enemies in Canaan.

Only two of the twelve spies kept their faith in God. Caleb and Joshua told the people that God was able to give them the land. "And Caleb said, Let us go up at once, and possess it; for we are well able to overcome it." Numbers 13:30. But the people would not listen to them.

Then God spake to Moses, and told him that Israel had been so rebellious that those who came out of Egypt should never enter the land of promise. They should wander in the wilderness forty years until they died, and when their children were grown He would bring them into the land.

But Caleb and Joshua had been faithful to God. These two were excepted, and of all the men that left Egypt, only these two should finally enter Canaan. The other ten spies, who had caused Israel to sin, were smitten by the plague, and died in the sight of all Israel.

All the next night Israel spent in mourning. They now realized what they had lost. But in the morning a new hope came to them. They would make up for their lack of courage. They would now go up and take the land.

The armies of Israel gathered, but Moses said to them, "Go not up, for the Lord is not among you." They had lost their opportunity, and if they went up God would not fight for them.

But the army of Israel was a vast multitude of over half a million solders. They now felt able to attack their enemies. So against the command of God they went up to battle with the armies of the Canaanites that had come out to meet them.

But the ark of God remained in camp, and so did Moses and Aaron, Caleb and Joshua. Without a leader, and forsaken of God, the army of Israel was defeated with great slaughter.

Then the Israelites turned back to the wilderness.

[137]

The Brazen Serpent.The Brazen Serpent.The Brazen Serpent.The Brazen Serpent.The Brazen Serpent.
THE Israelites wandered in the wilderness nearly forty years. Then, at the command of the Lord, they again turned their faces toward Canaan.

On this journey they were permitted to meet many difficulties, that their faith and trust in God might be tested. They were sometimes short of food to eat and water to drink, and as they neared the promised land great armies came out to destroy them. But the Lord helped them in every trouble, and gave them the victory over their enemies.

Part of their way lay through a hot, sandy desert, where they suffered from heat and thirst. But, instead of being patient, they rebelled against God, and found fault with Moses.

Moses holding up serpent on stick
The Brazen Serpent.
Then the Lord let serpents come into the camp, whose bite was like fire, and brought sure death. Some in almost every tent were bitten.

This punishment showed them their sin, and they came to Moses and said, "We have sinned, for we have spoken against the Lord, and against thee. Pray unto the Lord that He take away the serpents from us." Numbers 21:7-9.

In answer to the prayer of Moses the Lord told him to make a serpent of brass, and raise it up on a pole, so that all in the camp could see it. Those who were bitten were told to look at this Serpent and they would be healed. The serpent could not heal them, but to look required faith, and faith brought the healing power.

The Lord could have healed them with a word, but the[138]
[139] lesson must be complete. The lifting up of the serpent was to them a type of the lifting up of Christ on the cross, for through Him only could they receive pardon and relief from the consequences of sin. The brazen serpent was an object lesson to lead the children of Israel to look to Christ.

The Hebrews had the same Gospel, or good news of pardon and salvation through Christ, that we have. Speaking of them in the wilderness, the Apostle Paul says, "For unto us was the Gospel preached as well as unto them." Hebrews 4:2.

Every sacrifice they made for sin, every lamb slain, was to show their faith in "the Lamb of God, which taketh away the sin of the world." John 1:29. The blood of the offering was a type of the blood of Christ.

Jesus Christ is the great central figure of the Gospel. It was Christ who was with Israel in all their journey from Egypt to the promised land.

Christ was the "Spiritual Rock" which followed them. He was in the pillar of cloud by day, and in the pillar of fire by night. He was the "Angel" that went before Israel; for Jehovah said, "My name is in Him." (See Exodus 23:21, 22.) No being bears the name of God but His Son.

So, in the history of the world, it has not been as some have supposed, God the Father in the Old Testament, and Christ the Son in the New Testament. It has been Christ with His people all the way.

In the Old Testament Christ was their "Spiritual Rock." In the New Testament, "God was in Christ, reconciling the world unto Himself." 2 Corinthians 5:19.

Both the Father and the Son have ever worked for the salvation of man; but Christ has been the active agent in this work. It was God who "so loved the world that He gave His only begotten Son" for our redemption. It was Christ who made the terrible sacrifice for our salvation.

[140]

Crowd at river
The Israelites Crossing the Jordan.
[141]

Entering the Promised Land.Entering the Promised Land.Entering the Promised Land.Entering the Promised Land.Entering the Promised Land.Entering the Promised Land.
AS Israel neared the promised land, both Moses and Aaron died. Joshua was then made commander in the place of Moses.

43

Soon they came to the River Jordan, which they must cross. Here again the Lord made a way for them. He told Israel to go forward, and as the feet of the leaders touched the water, the river stopped flowing from above, and the bed of the stream was left dry. Then the people passed over on dry ground, as their fathers had crossed the Red Sea forty years before.

The book of Joshua tells of the battles that Israel fought with the inhabitants of the land of Canaan. These were very wicked nations, who were as bad as the people who lived before the flood. So the Lord used the armies of Israel to destroy those wicked people.

The first city overthrown was Jericho. This city had very strong and high walls, and the Hebrews were not able to break them down. But the Lord could do what man could not.

One day Joshua saw a man near the camp, with a sword drawn in his hand. "And Joshua went unto him and said, Art thou for us or for our adversaries?

"And he said, Nay; but as Captain of the host of the Lord am I come." Joshua 5:13-15. Then Joshua knew that it was Jesus Christ, for He is the Captain of the Lord's host.

[142]

Crowd with Joshua on rise
Joshua Commanding the Sun to Stand Still.
[143]

The Lord told Joshua what to do. Each day, for six days, all the army of Israel was to march around the city. The soldiers were to go ahead, the priests with the ark of God were to come next, and all the rest of the people were to follow.

On the seventh day they marched around the city seven times. "And it came to pass at the seventh time, when the priests blew with the trumpets, Joshua said unto the people, Shout; for the Lord hath given you the city." Joshua 6:16.

And when the people shouted, the walls of Jericho "fell down flat," and the soldiers went into the city and utterly destroyed it as the Lord had told them to do. This was to show to all nations that God was fighting for Israel.

The tenth chapter of Joshua also tells of a very wonderful battle between Israel and five of the kings of Canaan. All day the battle lasted, and God fought for Israel, sending down great hailstones upon their enemies. More were killed by these hailstones than were slain by the Israelites.

As the conflict raged, Joshua saw that the day would be too short to finish the battle. Then, led by the Spirit of God, he commanded the sun and moon to stand still until the work should be fully done.

"So the sun stood still in the midst of heaven, and hasted not to go down about a whole day. And there was no day like that before it or after it." Joshua 10:13, 14.

In this battle the armies of the wicked Canaanites were utterly destroyed, and their kings slain.

When the nations of Canaan were fully conquered, the land was divided up and given to the different tribes of Israel, as their home.

[144]

Soldiers with horns
Gideon's Three Hundred.
[145]

The Judges of Israel.The Judges of Israel.The Judges of Israel.The Judges of Israel.
AFTER the death of Joshua, Israel was governed by judges for many hundred years. Sometimes these judges were wicked men, and led the people into the worship of idols.

Then the Lord, although He still loved them, allowed their enemies to afflict them, that they might remember that He alone could save them from their foes and from sin.

Then when they returned to Him, confessed their sins, and put away their idols, He would choose good and wise men to be their judges. He would then go with their armies to battle, defeat their enemies, and deliver them.

At one time the armies of Midian afflicted Israel for seven years. At harvest time they would come "as grasshoppers for multitude," and take from Israel "all the increase of the earth." During these attacks the people fled to the dens, and caves, and strongholds of the mountains.

Then Israel cried to the Lord for help, and He raised up Gideon to deliver them. One day an angel appeared to him, as he was threshing grain in secret for fear of the invaders. And the angel told him that he was chosen to "save Israel from the hand of the Midianites."

Gideon then prepared food and brought it to the angel. He also asked for a sign that he might know that the words spoken by the angel came from the Lord. So instead of eating[146] the food, the angel said to Gideon, "Take the flesh and the unleavened cakes, and lay them upon this rock, and pour out the broth."

When Gideon had done as he was told, the angel touched the food with the rod in his hand, and fire came out of the rock and burned it. Then the angel disappeared, and Gideon knew that it was the Lord who had spoken to him.

And the Spirit of the Lord came upon Gideon, and he made a call for soldiers. But before he dared take command of the army that gathered, he asked for other signs that he might be sure that God had really chosen him and would go with him.

So one night he spread a fleece of wool on the floor, and asked the Lord that if He had chosen him to lead Israel, to let dew fall on the fleece, and the rest of the floor be dry. And in the morning he found it so.

The next night he asked that the dew might fall on the floor and dampen it, and the fleece remain dry. This also was done. Then Gideon knew that the Lord had called him to lead the armies of Israel.

Gideon's army numbered only thirty-two thousand men, but their enemies were "like grasshoppers for multitude." Yet the Lord told Gideon that his army was too large. The Lord would show all Israel that He would deliver them if they would trust him.

So Gideon was told to let all who were fearful go back to their homes. As a result, twenty-two thousand men returned, leaving only ten thousand.

Yet these were too many. The army must be so small that every one would know that it was God alone who gave the victory. So at the command of the Lord they were led to a brook to drink.

Those who kneeled down and drank were sent home. But there were three hundred men whose thoughts were only on[147] the work before them. They dipped up the water in their hands, and drank as they went on, with their faces toward the enemy.

These three hundred men were then armed for their work, and in a strange manner. Each man was given a trumpet, a pitcher, and a blazing torch hidden in the pitcher. This little army was then divided into three companies, and, in the darkness of night, approached the hosts of Midian from three sides.

At a signal from Gideon, all three companies gave a blast of their trumpets to awaken the sleeping enemy. Then they broke the pitchers and let their torches flame up, and gave the battle cry,—"The sword of the Lord, and of Gideon." To the Midianites it appeared that they were surrounded by a great army.

In their fear they fled for life. They mistook their own companions for enemies, and killed one another. The news of the victory spread, and thousands of Israel joined in pursuit of their retreating foes, and the great army of Midianites was utterly destroyed.

The strongest and most wonderful Judge of Israel was Samson. According to instruction given his mother from the Lord, he was a "Nazarite" from his birth. This meant that he was to drink no wine, and the hair of his head was never to be cut.

45

As he grew up, the Lord gave him wonderful strength. One day as he was passing through a vineyard of the Philistines, a young lion met him. He had no weapons with him, but with his bare hands he tore the lion and killed him.

Soon after this a great army of Philistines came out against Israel. "And the Spirit of the Lord came mightily upon Samson." His only weapon was the jaw bone of an ass; but with this he defeated the whole army of the Philistines, and slew a thousand of them.

[148]

Samson carrying a gate up a hill in the sunset
Samson Carrying the Gates of Gaza.
[149]

Here was another lesson of what the Lord could do for His people. Gideon had three hundred men when he fought the hosts of Midian; but at this time one man alone won the battle against an army of the Philistines.

At another time Samson stayed part of a night in a city of the Philistines, called Gaza. And the dwellers in Gaza shut the gates, and set men to watch them, so that when he should come out they might kill him.

But before morning Samson arose, tore down the great gate of the city, carried it on his shoulders to a hill, and left it there.

All the wonderful things that Samson did, and how he finally died, a prisoner to the Philistines, are recorded in Judges 13-16.

boy Samuel kneeling to pray
The Child Samuel.
About fifty years after Samson's death, Samuel was born, who was to be both a judge and a prophet. His mother was a good woman. The Bible says, she "lent him to the Lord as long as he liveth." 1 Samuel 11:28.

Eli was priest at this time in the temple of the Lord, and "the child Samuel ministered unto the Lord before Eli."

While Samuel was a small boy, it came to pass one night, ere the lamp of God went out in the temple of the Lord, where the ark of God was, and Samuel was laid down to sleep, that the Lord called Samuel, and he answered, "Here am I," thinking Eli had called him.

Three times this occurred. Then Samuel said, "Speak, Lord; for Thy servant heareth."

Let us answer the Lord as did Samuel. He speaks to each of us in His word, the Bible.

[150]

Two men in wilderness
The Parting of David and Jonathan.
[151]

The Kings of Israel.The Kings of Israel.The Kings of Israel.
UNTIL the days of Samuel, Israel was not governed by kings. Jehovah had promised to be their Ruler and King. Had they been true to Him they would have been prospered and given every needed blessing.

But the people wanted to be like the nations around them. So the elders came to Samuel and said, "Make us a king to judge us like all the nations."

Samuel was a prophet of the Lord, and had been the judge of Israel for many years. Their demand for a king displeased him, for he felt that the people had rejected him.

But the Lord told Samuel to do as they asked, "for they have not rejected thee, but they have rejected Me." And the Lord chose Saul, of the tribe of Benjamin, to be king.

At the command of the Lord, Samuel anointed Saul as king. A little later he called the people together and presented their new-made king to them. And they shouted, "God save the king!"

But Saul soon became proud, and many times refused to obey the Lord. Then the Lord rejected Saul and chose David, a young shepherd boy, to be king when Saul should die. And Samuel anointed David to be king in the place of Saul.

crowd of people in cliffs
David and Saul at the Cave.
When Saul heard of this he was very angry, and tried[152]
[153] many times to kill David. Saul wanted his son Jonathan to be king when he died. How foolish it was for Saul to try to kill David, when God had said he should be king over Israel!

So David fled from Saul, and for many years lived among strangers, and in the dens and caves of the mountains. But Saul hunted him so many times that David had to change his hiding place very often.

One time Saul lay down to sleep in the very cave where David was hidden, not knowing he was there. Some of the men who were with David wanted him to kill Saul, but he would not do it. He only crept up to the king and cut off a piece of the robe which he wore.

When the king had gone, David called to him and showed him the piece he had cut from his garment. Saul saw at once that David could have killed him as easily as he cut a piece from his garment.

Then Saul promised David that he would not again try to destroy him. But David did not trust his promises; and it was well he did not, for Saul was soon hunting him as wickedly as before.

Notwithstanding David was hated by Saul, his son Jonathan loved David. They were as brothers to each other. Jonathan was a true servant of God. He was always true to David, and whenever he could aid him in escaping from his father, he did so, notwithstanding he knew that David was to be made king instead of himself. This shows that he was one of the most generous and lovable characters recorded in the Bible.

Finally there was a great battle between Saul's army and the Philistines. In this battle Jonathan was slain, and Saul fell on his own sword and killed himself.

Soon after this David was made king. In most things he was a good king, and obeyed the Lord and ruled Israel well. He was a great warrior, and subdued the enemies of his people.

[154]

pomp
Solomon and the Queen of Sheba
[155]

At the death of David, his son Solomon was made king. He was a very wise man and a good king. It was he who built at Jerusalem the wonderful temple for the service of the Lord.

The wisdom and riches of Solomon were so wonderful that his fame was spread abroad in all the earth. And the queen of Sheba, in Arabia, came to see if all the reports she had heard were true.

And the queen asked Solomon hard questions; but he was able to answer every one of them. She was then shown the riches and wonderful works of Solomon.

When ready to return to her own land she told Solomon that she had heard wonderful reports about him and his kingdom, but she had not believed them. Now, she said, "Mine eyes have seen it; and, behold, the one-half of the greatness of thy wisdom was not told me." 2 Chronicles 9.

After the days of Solomon, Israel was ruled by many kings. Some of them were good, and their rule brought the blessing of God to their people. But many were wicked men who led Israel into sin and idolatry. Then the Lord could not protect them, and their enemies would afflict them.

The history of Israel is a sorrowful story. God wanted to bless them and make them the light of the world. He wanted to show the whole world what wonderful things He would do for those who were faithful to Him. But they preferred their own way, and in consequence perished as a nation.

The apostle Paul says that "all these things happened unto them for ensamples; and they are written for our admonition, upon whom the ends of the world are come." 1 Corinthians 10:11.

[156]

light falling on Daniel in lion's den
Daniel in the Den of Lions
[157]

The Prophets of Israel.The Prophets of Israel.The Prophets of Israel.The Prophets of Israel.The Prophets of Israel.The Prophets of Israel.

AFTER Samuel, the sixteen prophets whose writings bear their names in the Bible, may be classified as follows:—

(1) Those before Israel's Babylonian captivity, namely: Jonah, Joel, Amos, Hosea, Isaiah, Micah.

(2) Those near to, and during the captivity: Nahum, Zephaniah, Habakkuk, Jeremiah, Daniel, Obadiah, Ezekiel.

(3) Those after the return from the captivity in Babylon: Haggai, Zachariah, Malachi.

The books which bear these names in our Bible are not arranged in the order in which they were written; but in the order of their supposed importance. But man can not tell which part of God's word is most valuable. "All scripture is given by inspiration of God."

Peter says that "the prophecy came not in old time by the will of man; but holy men of God spake as they were moved by the Holy Ghost." 2 Peter 1:21.

We will refer to a few prophecies which have been fulfilled:

Isaiah mentions by name the Persian prince, Cyrus, 200 years before he was born, and tells what he should do. Compare Isaiah 44:28 with Ezra 1:1, and notice the dates in the margin of your Bible.

Isaiah also foretold and described the sufferings of Jesus. Compare the fifty-third chapter of Isaiah with Luke 22:37; John 1:10, 11; Matthew 8:17; 1 Peter 2:24, 25; Acts 8:32-38; Luke 22:37; Matthew 27:57-60.

[158]

Daniel in front of the king
Daniel Interpreting the King's Dream.

Forty-seven of the sixty-six chapters in Isaiah are referred to in the New Testament, and Jesus twice mentioned Isaiah by name. Matthew 13:14; Matthew 15:37.

Jeremiah prophesied that Jerusalem should be destroyed, and that during the siege the famine should be so great that the Jews should "eat the flesh of their sons and the flesh of their daughters." Jeremiah 19:9.

This prophecy was given six hundred and five years before Christ, and it was fulfilled when the Roman army surrounded Jerusalem, A. D. 70, thirty-six years after the crucifixion of Jesus.

Some of the most wonderful of the prophecies are in the book of Daniel. The history of the world since his time is given plainly in chapters two, seven and eight.

In the second chapter the Lord foretold, by a dream, what should come to pass from that time to the end of the world.

Daniel, a prophet of the Lord, was given wisdom to tell the[159] king his dream, which he had forgotten, and also its meaning, after the false prophets had confessed that they could not do so.

48

Daniel said: "There is a God in heaven that revealeth secrets, and maketh known to the king Nebuchadnezzar what shall be in the latter days." Daniel 2:28.

So the interpretation is for us, because "the secret things belong unto the Lord our God; but those things which are revealed belong unto us and to our children." Deuteronomy 29:29.

Prophecy is history told in advance. The Lord is the only one who can do this without making a mistake.

Turn to Daniel 2:31-36, and read the dream. Verses 37 to 45 interpret it plainly, showing that the four parts of the image mean four great kingdoms.

History tells us that the Babylonian kingdom, symbolized by the head of gold, was conquered B. C. 538 (five hundred and thirty-eight years before the time of Christ), by the Medo-Persians, represented by the breast and arms of silver. Cyrus was their general.

The Medo-Persians were overcome by the Grecians, under Alexander, 331 B. C. The brass thighs of the image represent their kingdom.

The Romans, "strong as iron," signified by the legs of iron, subdued the Grecians in the year 168 B. C.

The feet and toes of the image represent the ten parts into which the Roman empire was divided between the years 351 and 476 after the birth of Christ.

These parts of Rome exist in Europe to-day, under the names, England, Germany, France, Spain, Italy, etc., and will continue separate (see verse 43) until the kingdom of Christ is set up, represented by the stone "cut out of the mountain without hands," which "shall break in pieces and consume all these kingdoms, and shall stand for ever." Jesus said, "Blessed are the meek, for they shall inherit the earth."

[160]

Smiths converting swords
Swords and Plowshares, Spears and Pruning Hooks.
[161]

What the Bible Says About War.They that take the Sword shall Perish with the Sword....What the Bible Says About War.What the Bible Says About War.
THE great Teacher said, "Love your enemies, bless them that curse you, do good to them that hate you, and pray for them which despitefully use you." Matthew 5:9, 39-44.

When everybody does this, there will be no war. All will be righteous; for "love is the fulfilling of the law," God's standard of right-doing.

But no person can love everybody without a change of heart. "Ye must be born again," said Jesus. This change, or new life, comes by believing that God will change us. It is only when we stop believing right that we stop doing right.

If the world would believe, the world would be converted, or changed; but the parable of the tares and the wheat (Matthew 13:36-43), and what Jesus said about the "many" in the broad way and the "few" in the narrow way (Matt. 7:13, 14), show that "many are called, but few chosen."

Yet thousands of people are prophesying "peace and safety" (1 Thessalonians 5:1-5), forgetting that "evil men and seducers shall wax worse and worse, deceiving and being deceived" (2 Timothy 3:13), and that the "tares," or sinners, are finally to be destroyed instead of being changed over into wheat. "Ye will not come unto Me," said Jesus.

One of the prophecies of Isaiah (2:2-5) says that "many people" "in the last days" shall talk about peace as if it were coming soon by the conversion of the world. The marginal reading of Isaiah 2:16, calls such talk "pictures of desire," and says they shall "be brought low" (verse 12).

Verses three to five tell what the "people" are saying. Verses six to twenty-two are the prophet's declarations because of what the people have said. He foretells destruction for those who do not repent, the same as does the prophet Joel. It will be a time of general war. Here are the people's sayings and the Lord's

49

sayings, side by side. They are direct opposites; yet both refer to "the last days," when "the day of the Lord is near:"

"It shall come to pass in THE LAST DAYS that . . . MANY PEOPLE shall say, Come ye, and let us go up to the mountain of the Lord, to the house of the God of Jacob; and he will teach us of his ways, and we will walk in his paths: . . .

"And he shall judge among the nations, and shall rebuke many people: and they shall beat their swords into plowshares, and their spears into pruninghooks: nation shall not lift up sword against nation, neither shall they learn war any more.

"O house of Jacob, come ye and let us walk in the light of the Lord." Isaiah 2:2-5.

Proclaim ye this among the Gentiles. Prepare war, wake up the mighty men, let all the men of war draw near; let them come up:

"Beat your plowshares into swords, and your pruninghooks into spears: let the weak say I am strong. . . . Put ye in the sickle, for the harvest is ripe: come, . . . for their WICKEDNESS is great.

"Multitudes, multitudes in the valley of decision: for the day of the Lord is near in the valley of decision." Joel 3:9-16.

The DAY OF THE LORD "shall come as A DESTRUCTION from the Almighty." Isaiah 13:6-11.

[162]

John preaching to crowd
John the Baptist by the Jordan.
[163]

The Birth of Jesus.The Birth of Jesus.The Birth of Jesus.The Birth of Jesus.
"THERE was a man sent from God, whose name was John.

"The same came for a witness, to bear witness of the Light, that all men through Him might believe.

"He was not that Light, but was sent to bear witness of that Light." John 1:6-8.

"As it is written in the prophets, Behold, I send My Messenger before Thy face, which shall prepare Thy way before Thee.

"The voice of one crying in the wilderness, Prepare ye the way of the Lord, make His paths straight.

"John did baptize in the wilderness, and preach the baptism of repentance for the remission of sins.

"And there went out unto him all the land of Judea, and they of Jerusalem, and were all baptized of him in the river of Jordan, confessing their sins.

"And John was clothed with camel's hair, and with a girdle of a skin about his loins; and he did eat locusts and wild honey;

"And preached, saying, There cometh One mightier than I after me, the latchet of whose shoes I am not worthy to stoop down and unloose.

"I indeed have baptized you with water; but He shall baptize you with the Holy Ghost." Mark 1:2-8.

crowd seeing bright light in distance
The Wise Men Following the Star.
In ancient times, when a king made a visit to another country, he sent messengers before him. These messengers would see that there was a good path for him to travel, and[164]
[165] that the people where he was going were ready to receive him.

John the Baptist was God's messenger, sent to arouse the people of this world, and prepare them to receive Jesus when He should come to visit them.

Before Jesus came to this earth He was a great King in heaven. Paul says He was "equal with God." Philippians 2:6.

We can never understand how the Son of God, the great King of heaven, could come to this earth as a babe. This is one of God's great mysteries.

But he did come in just this way. He was born in a manger in Bethlehem. Coming in this humble manner, the priests and rulers of Israel were not ready to receive this Babe as their Saviour. They were looking for Him to come as a great King, in pomp and splendor.

But there were on the plains of Bethlehem some humble shepherds who were looking and waiting for the promised Messiah. To them angels were sent to tell of the birth of Jesus.

And the angel said, "Ye shall find the babe wrapped in swaddling clothes, lying in a manger." And they went to Bethlehem in haste, and found the infant Jesus as the angel had told them.

God meant that others, as well as the Jews, should know that the Saviour had come to begin His work on earth. Away off in the Eastern country there were wise men who had read the prophecies about the Messiah, and believed that He would soon appear.

at the stable
The Shepherds Worship Jesus.
One night these men saw a wonderfully bright star in the sky, moving toward the land of Judea. They believed this to be a sign that the Messiah had come. So they followed the star, and it brought them to the manger in Bethlehem.

"And when they were come into the house, they saw the[166] young child with Mary His mother, and fell down and worshiped Him; and when they had opened their treasures, they presented unto Him gifts; gold, and frankincense, and myrrh.

"And being warned of God in a dream that they should not return to Herod, they departed into their own country another way.

"And when they were departed, behold, the angel of the Lord appeareth to Joseph in a dream, saying, Arise, and take the young child and His mother, and flee into Egypt, and be thou there until I bring thee word: for Herod will seek the young child to destroy Him."

Find the second chapter of Matthew, and read about the flight into Egypt, and why they finally went to Nazareth, in Galilee, instead of to a city of Judea. Verses 15 and 23 tell the reason.

[167]

The Childhood of Jesus.The Childhood of Jesus.The Childhood of Jesus.
THE early life of Jesus was spent in Nazareth, a small city in the northern part of Palestine. His parents were very poor, and He had only what poor children have.

His father was a carpenter, and Christ learned the carpenter's trade and worked with him. From His earliest days He was a pattern of obedience and industry. He was used to a life of hardship and toil, and can comfort all those who must work for a living.

Of the childhood of Jesus it is written, "The child grew, and waxed strong in spirit, filled with wisdom; and the grace of God was upon Him." Luke 2:40.

The mother of Jesus was His first earthly teacher. From her lips, and by reading the prophecies, He was taught of heavenly things and of His mission to this world.

Jesus in the temple
\Jesus among the Teachers of the Law.

51

The wonderful truths which He Himself had spoken to Moses and the prophets, He was now taught by His mother. The Holy Spirit gave her wisdom to teach Him aright. All parents should teach their children as Jesus was taught, that every child may obtain knowledge as Jesus did.

Jesus left all His glory and power when He came to earth as a babe. He took His place by the side of the fallen men of earth. He came "in the likeness of sinful flesh." He was subject to all the temptations and weakness of our fallen race.

Jesus and Joseph working
Jesus in the Carpenter Shop.
Yet by the power of God He was kept from yielding to[168]
[169] the temptations which surrounded Him. This power He gained by earnest prayer to His Father in Heaven. This power every child and man can obtain in the same way.

In His humble life, as the child of poor parents, He faithfully did His part of the work. Ever obedient and cheerful, He was as a pleasant sunbeam in the home circle.

Once a year His parents went up to Jerusalem to attend the passover. When Jesus was twelve years of age He went up with them.

When the feast was over, Joseph and Mary started for home with a company of friends, but Jesus remained in Jerusalem. They supposed He was in the company, and did not miss Him until they had journeyed a whole day. Then they turned back to find Him.

"And it came to pass, that after three days, they found Him in the temple, sitting in the midst of the doctors, both hearing them and asking them questions." Luke 2:46. These doctors were learned men in the Scriptures, yet they were astonished at the questions and answers of Jesus. They soon saw that He had a deeper knowledge of the Word of God than they had, although He was so young.

Jesus seemed to know the Scriptures from beginning to end. He repeated them in such a way that their true meaning shone[170] out. His knowledge of the Scriptures made them ashamed.

"Though Christ seemed like a child that was seeking help from those who knew a great deal more than He did, yet He was bringing light to their minds in every word He spoke." While appearing to instruct Jesus, these doctors were asking questions and learning Bible truths which they did not understand.

And while Jesus was thus teaching others, "He Himself was receiving light and knowledge about His own work and mission in the world; for it is plainly stated that Christ 'grew in knowledge.'"

When Mary found Him she said, "Son, why hast Thou thus dealt with us? Behold, Thy father and I have sought Thee sorrowing." And Jesus answered, "How is it that ye sought me? Wist ye not that I must be about My Father's business?"

His parents could not understand Him then, but when He began His ministry it was plain to them.

"And He went down with them, and came to Nazareth, and was subject unto them; but His mother kept all these sayings in her heart. And Jesus increased in wisdom and stature, and in favor with God and man." Luke 2:41-53.

[171]

The Early Ministry of Jesus.The Early Ministry of Jesus.The Early Ministry of Jesus.The Early Ministry of Jesus.The Early Ministry of Jesus.The Early Ministry of Jesus.
WHEN Jesus was about thirty years of age, He went to be baptized by John in the River Jordan. He was not baptized because He was a sinner, but to set an example for all to follow.

When He came out of the water the Holy Spirit, in the form of a dove, descended from Heaven upon Him. Then the voice of God was heard, saying "This is My beloved Son, in whom I am well pleased."

The descent of the dove upon Christ was His anointing for the work of the ministry that was before Him. From the Jordan the Spirit led Him into the wilderness, where He fasted forty days, and where the devil tempted Him in many ways, as recorded in Matthew 4:1-11.

From the wilderness He returned to the Jordan, and began to choose His disciples. We next hear of Him at the marriage at Cana of Galilee, where He performed the wonderful miracle of turning water into wine.

Soon after this, Jesus went to Jerusalem to attend the feast of the passover. As He entered the temple where God was worshiped, He found the court filled with cattle, sheep, and birds, for sale to those who would buy sacrifices for their sins.

Cheating and robbery were carried on in the very temple court. Even priests and rulers were engaged in this unholy traffic. As Jesus stands on the temple steps His eye views the whole scene. His countenance changes, and all seem compelled to look upon Him.

[172]

Jesus swinging a whip
Jesus Drives the Buyers and Sellers from the Temple.
[173]

All trading ceased, and there was silence in the temple court. Then, raising a whip of small cords, He cried, "Take these things hence; make not My Father's house an house of merchandise." John 2:16.

Priests, and rulers, and merchants fled in terror from the temple. They could not endure the look on His face nor the power of His voice. The divine power had flashed through the humanity of Christ.

After a time the crowd that had fled at the words of Jesus came slowly back; but what a change had taken place! Instead of unholy trade, they saw the Saviour healing the sick who were pressing around Him.

On every side was heard the urgent, pitiful appeals, "Master, bless me." All were healed who came to Him. The lame were made to walk, the dumb to speak, and the blind to see.

The mothers brought their children to be healed and blessed. The little sufferers were returned to their mother's arms with the bloom of health and the smile of happiness on their faces.

Jesus loved the children because they were so pure and innocent and simple in their ways. He took them as an example of the purity and simplicity that should show in the lives of those who should follow Him.

One day some mothers brought their children to Jesus, hoping that He would bless them. But He had worked a long time, and needed rest. So His disciples rebuked the mothers, and told them not to trouble the Master.

"But when Jesus saw it, He was much displeased, and said unto them, Suffer the little children to come unto Me, and forbid them not; for of such is the kingdom of God." Mark 10:14.

The pen of Julia Gill has given the following beautiful description of this scene:—

[174]

Jesus and crowd iwth children
Jesus Blessing the Children.
[175]

Christ and the Little Ones.
"THE Master has come over Jordan,"
Said Hannah, the mother, one day,
"He is healing the people who throng Him,
With a touch of His finger, they say.
"And now I shall carry the children—
Little Rachel, and Samuel, and John,
I shall carry the baby, Esther,
For the Lord to look upon."
The father looked at her kindly,
But he shook his head and smiled;

53

"Now, who but a doting mother
Would think of a thing so wild?
"If the children were tortured by demons,
Or dying of fever, 'twere well,
Or had they the taint of the leper,
Like many in Israel."
"Nay, do not hinder me, Nathan—
I feel such a burden of care;
If I carry it to the Master,
Perhaps I shall leave it there.
"If he lays His hand on the children,
My heart will be lighter, I know,
For a blessing for ever and ever
Will follow them as they go."
So over the hills to Judah,
Along the vine-rows green,
With Esther asleep on her bosom,
And Rachel her brothers between,
'Mong the people who hung on His teaching,
Or waited His touch and His word,
Through the row of proud Pharisees listening,
She pressed to the feet of the Lord.
"Now, why shouldst thou hinder the Master,"
Said Peter, "with children like these?
Seest not how, from morning till evening,
He teacheth, and healeth disease?"
Then Christ said, "Forbid not the children—
Permit them to come unto Me."
And He took in His arms little Esther,
And Rachel He set on His knee;
And the heavy heart of the mother
Was lifted all earth-care above;
And He laid His hands on the brothers,
And blest them with tenderest love.
As He said of the babes in His bosom,
"Of such is the kingdom of heaven,"
New strength for all duty and trial
That hour to her spirit was given.
[176]

Martha, Jesus and Mary
At the Home of Mary and Martha
[177]

Jesus in the Home.Jesus in the Home.Jesus in the Home.Jesus in the Home.Jesus in the Home.
ON earth Jesus had no home of His own. He said of Himself, "The foxes have holes, and the birds of the air have nests; but the Son of man hath not where to lay His head." See Matthew 8:20.

He never remained long in one place. We read of His beautiful teachings and wonderful miracles in all parts of Palestine. At one time He is on the shore of the Sea of Galilee. At another time He is in Jerusalem, cleansing the temple and healing the sick. Then He is by Jacob's well, in Samaria, teaching the people of Sychar the way to everlasting life.

He had no home of His own, but many were glad to receive Him as a loved and honored guest. When in these homes He more than repaid them for their care, by the beautiful lessons He taught, and the sorrows He comforted.

And we can have Jesus in our homes to-day just as truly as they had Him when He was on earth. If we invite Him, He will come into our homes and dwell with us, and teach us, and help us in all our trials, and comfort us in all our sorrows.

In the little town of Bethany, near Jerusalem, was the home of Lazarus and his sisters Mary and Martha. At this pleasant home the Saviour was always welcome. This whole family believed in Jesus and His mission, and eagerly listened to the words which He spake.

[178]

In this peaceful home Jesus often found rest. When weary, and feeling the need of human sympathy, He was glad to escape from the throngs of people, and the contentions of the wicked Pharisees, for the quiet and peace of this humble home.

At the time of His first visit to Bethany, His disciples came with Him to the home of Lazarus. Here He had no enemies to watch his words, and He taught the great truths of the gospel plainly, and not in parables.

Prizing these lessons, Mary sat at the feet of Jesus, an eager listener to the wonderful words of life. But Martha was busy preparing food for the guests. She was very anxious that they should be comfortably cared for.

Martha felt that her sister was not helping in the work as she ought, and came to Christ, and said, "Lord, dost Thou not care that my sister hath left me to serve alone? bid her therefore that she help me."

But Jesus answered, "Martha, Martha, thou art careful and troubled about many things; but one thing is needful; and Mary hath chosen that good part which shall not be taken away from her." Luke 10:40, 41.

The most important thing in this world is to learn the great lessons which Jesus teaches. There is need for the Marthas with their zeal and carefulness for the work and servants of God. But first they should, like Mary, learn at the feet of Jesus.

"Happy the home where Jesus' name
Is sweet to ev'ry ear;
Where children early lisp His fame,
And parents hold Him dear.
"Lord, may we in our homes agree,
This blessed peace to gain;
Unite our hearts in love to Thee,
And love to all will reign."
[179]

The Miracles of Jesus.The Miracles of Jesus.The Miracles of Jesus.
DURING His mission on earth, Jesus performed many wonderful miracles. He healed the sick, gave sight to the blind, made the deaf to hear, cleansed the lepers, raised the dead, stilled the storm, and did many other wonderful works.

At one time Jesus had been teaching all day in a desert place. As the night came on the disciples asked Him to send the people away that they might go into the villages and buy food to eat.

But Jesus answered, "Give ye them to eat." They were astonished at this, for there were five thousand people to be fed, and they had only five loaves and two small fishes.

Then Jesus took the loaves and fishes and blessed them, and divided them among the people. "And they did all eat, and were filled. And they took up twelve baskets full of the fragments, and of the fishes," Mark 6:39-44

At another time four of the disciples fished all night on the Lake of Gennesaret, or Galilee, and had caught nothing. And Jesus said to Peter, "Launch out into the deep, and let down your net for a draught."

But Peter was discouraged, and said, "Master, we have toiled all the night and have taken nothing; nevertheless at Thy word I will let down the net. And when they had this done, they inclosed a great multitude of fishes; and their net brake." Luke 5:1-7.

[180]

Jesus and fishermen and lots of fish
The Net Full of Fishes.

55

Then Peter and Andrew called to James and John to come with their boat and help them. And both boats were filled with the fish.

Some time after this miracle, Jesus and the disciples were crossing this same lake, and a terrible storm arose. But Jesus was lying asleep on one of the hard seats of the boat.

The disciples worked hard to save the boat; but when it began to fill with water, they awoke Him, and said, "Master, Master, we perish." And the Saviour rebuked the storm, and it ceased, and the waters became still.

Every miracle performed by Jesus had a lesson for us. These miracles show that the Lord can control every element for the good of His people and work. They also show that He can provide for all our wants.

Wherever Jesus went, the sick and the suffering were brought to Him, and He never turned them away. By a touch the blind received their sight. By a word the deaf were made to hear, and the lame to walk.

To the appeal of the lepers He said, "I will, be thou clean," and they were cured of their loathsome disease. At His command the devils were cast out, and those having all manner of diseases were healed.

All sickness and suffering are the result of sin. When the same dear hand that healed the sick on earth shall destroy sin, all sickness and suffering shall be forever ended.

Among the many miracles of Jesus, even the dead were raised to life. The daughter of Jairus, a ruler in Israel, was sick, and before Jesus reached her she died. Yet He took her by the hand, and said, "Damsel, I say unto thee, arise." And she was raised to life and perfect health. See Mark 5:22-43.

The son of the widow of Nain was raised from the dead as he was being taken to the place of burial. See Luke 7:11-15.

Jesus healing
The Mighty Healer.
But the greatest exhibition of divine power was in the raising of Lazarus, who had been dead four days. He had been dead so long that no one even thought of his being raised.

But when the stone was rolled away, Jesus cried, "Lazarus, come forth!" At the call of the Life-giver, he that had been dead came to the door of the sepulcher. And Jesus said, "Loose him, and let him go." These miracles show that Jesus can break the power of death. When He shall again come to this earth He will bring the final reward to His people. See Revelation 22:12.

Paul based his future hope on the resurrection. "For if the dead rise not, then is not Christ raised; and if Christ be not raised, your faith is vain, ye are yet in your sins. Then they also which have fallen asleep in Christ are perished." 1 Cor. 15:16-18.

Moses.Moses.Moses.Moses.
MUCH of the teaching of our Saviour was made plain by the use of parables, or object lessons. He took the things of every-day life, with which all were familiar, to illustrate the truths of eternal life.

"And He spake this parable unto certain which trusted in themselves that they were righteous, and despised others:

"Two men went up into the temple to pray; the one a Pharisee, and the other a publican.

"The Pharisee stood and prayed thus with himself, God, I thank Thee, that I am not as other men are, extortioners, unjust, adulterers, or even as this publican. I fast twice in the week, I give tithes of all I possess.

"And the publican, standing afar off, would not lift up so much as his eyes unto Heaven, but smote upon his breast, saying, God be merciful to me a sinner." Luke 18:9-13.

praying to be seen and praying to be heard
The Pharisee and the Publican
Our own righteousness is nothing but "filthy rags." Our own good deeds can never save us. Prayer is simply coming to God as our Father. It is telling Him of our needs, and thanking Him for His blessings.

The Pharisee felt no need, and so received no blessing. The publican knew he was a sinner, and asked for the mercy of God. Hence he went from the temple forgiven, "justified," made just before God. His record was made clean on the books of Heaven.

In another parable Jesus said, "There was a certain rich[184] [185] man, which was clothed in purple and fine linen, and fared sumptuously every day.

rich man having poor man thrown out
The Rich Man and Lazarus.
"And there was a certain beggar named Lazarus, which was laid at his gate, full of sores, and desiring to be fed with the crumbs which fell from the rich man's table." See Luke 16:19-31.

The rich man died and was punished, because he had not made God his hope and trust. But Lazarus, although poor and afflicted, had been a servant of the Most High God. He also died, but received the glorious reward which God has in store for all who obey Him.

This parable teaches that riches are no sign of God's favor; neither does poverty indicate that one is rejected of God. At another time a lawyer asked Jesus, "Who is my neighbor?"

Jesus answered with a parable. A man traveling from[186] Jerusalem to Jericho was met by thieves, who beat him, and robbed him, and left him, supposing he was dead.

A priest came that way, but passed by on the other side of the road. A Levite also came and looked at him, and then went away without giving aid. But at last, one of the Samaritans (a people despised by the Jews) came along. When he saw the wounded man, he bound up his wounds, lifted him onto his beast, took him to an inn, and cared for him.

Then Jesus asked, "which now of these three, thinkest thou, was neighbor unto him that fell among the thieves?" And the lawyer could only answer, "He that showed mercy on him." Then Jesus said, "Go, and do thou likewise." See Luke 10:25-37.

Samaritan holidng injured man on horse
The Good Samaritan.
Our neighbor is any human being in need. A man despised may be living out the principles taught by Christ, better than the ones who despise him.

[187]

The Death and Resurrection of Jesus.The Death and Resurrection of Jesus.The Death and Resurrection of Jesus.The Death and Resurrection of Jesus.
AFTER three years and a half of ministry, Jesus came to Jerusalem to eat the last passover. From the supper room He went with His disciples to the Garden of Gethsemane. Jesus knew that the time for His suffering and death had now come, and He went to the garden for one last season of prayer to His Father.

We can never understand the terrible sufferings of Christ in Gethsemane. He was to suffer for the sins of the world. He must feel the displeasure which God has for sin.

So great was His mental agony that drops of blood, like sweat, stood upon His face. Three times He prayed to the Father for strength and submission for the awful trial before Him.

After each prayer He came to the disciples for sympathy; but each time found them asleep. Had they watched and prayed with the Master, they, too, would have received strength for the trial and sorrow before them.

57

After the last prayer, He said to the disciples, "Rise, let us be going; behold he is at hand that doth betray Me." Matthew 26:45, 46. They were then met by the throng that had come to take Jesus, and Judas betrayed His Master with a kiss.

Jesus praying with an angel watching
In Gethsemane.
That same night Jesus was examined before the high priests[188]
[189] and the Sanhedrim, and in the morning He was taken before Pilate for condemnation. Pilate was a Roman governor, and no one could be put to death unless he commanded it.

When Pilate saw Jesus, he did not believe he was a criminal. He saw a man of noble, dignified bearing, with no appearance of crime about Him.

Angel talking to Pilate's wife, Jesus in backtround in crowd
The Dream of Pilate's Wife
But men had been hired by the priests to testify falsely against Jesus. Pilate listened to them, and then questioned the Saviour. He then gave his decision, "I find no fault in the Man." Pilate wished to release Him: but the priests were determined that he should be put to death.

Then Pilate sent Jesus bound to Herod, for Herod was ruler of Galilee, and the home of Jesus had been in that country. The soldiers mocked and derided Him, and then Herod sent Him back to Pilate.

Pilate was angry when Jesus was brought back to Him for final trial. So he said, "I will therefore chastise Him and let Him go." But the priests would not consent, and all cried out, "Away with this man." Nothing less than the death of Jesus would pacify them.

At this time God sent a warning to Pilate. An angel troubled the mind of Pilate's wife, and she sent word to her husband, "Have thou nothing to do with that just Man; for I have suffered many things this day in a dream because of Him." Matthew 27:19.

But Pilate feared to displease the Jews. So he washed his hands before the people, to show that he would not be responsible for the death of Jesus. And yet Pilate condemned Him to death, and He was taken to Calvary and crucified between two thieves.

Tender, loving hands took Him down from the cruel cross, and laid Him away in Joseph's new tomb. But the tomb could not hold Him.

[190]

angel in tomb talking to women: He is not here; for He is risen.angel in tomb talking to women: He is not here; for He is risen.
[191]

Early on the morning of the first day of the week, a powerful angel was sent from the courts of Heaven. The stone was rolled away from the tomb, and the angel cried with a loud voice, "Jesus, Thou Son of God, come forth, Thy Father calls Thee!" And Christ came from the tomb, a conquerer over sin, Satan, death, and the grave.

When the women came that morning, to care for the body of Jesus, they found a shining angel at the tomb. And he said to them, "Fear not ye; for I know that ye seek Jesus, which was crucified.

"He is not here; for He is risen, as He said. Come and see the place where the Lord lay. And go quickly and tell His disciples that He is risen from the dead; and, behold, He goeth before you into Galilee; there shall ye see Him; lo, I have told you.

"And they departed quickly from the sepulcher with fear and great joy; and did run to bring His disciples word." Matthew 28:1-8.

[192]

The Dominion Restored.The Dominion Restored.The Dominion Restored.The Dominion Restored.The Dominion Restored.

AFTER the resurrection Jesus appeared to His disciples at different times and places. They were thus strengthened for the work that was before them.

At His last visit, forty days after the resurrection, He walked with them from Jerusalem to the Mount of Olives. Here He gave the blessed promise, so dear to every child of God, "Lo, I am with you alway, even unto the end of the world." Matthew 28:20.

And then, with hands raised in blessing, He rose from among them. As they gazed upward, "a cloud [of heavenly angels] received Him out of their sight."

Had they lost their Saviour forever? Oh, no! Two shining angels had been sent to comfort them, and said, "Ye men of Galilee, why stand ye gazing up into Heaven? this same Jesus, which is taken up from you into Heaven, shall so come in like manner as ye have seen Him go into Heaven." Acts 1:9-11.

Jesus Himself has said, "I will come again, and receive you unto Myself; that where I am, there ye may be also." John 14:1-3.

The angels told the disciples that He would "so come in like manner as ye have seen Him go into Heaven." He ascended bodily, in plain sight of the disciples. When He returns, "every eye shall see Him." Revelation 1:7.

Jesus ascending in a cloud
The Ascension.
Paul, in describing Christ's second coming, says, "For the[193] Lord Himself shall descend from Heaven with a shout, with the voice of the Archangel, and with the trump of God; and the dead in Christ shall rise first. Then we which are alive and remain shall be caught up together with them in the clouds, to meet the Lord in the air; and so shall we ever be with the Lord." 1 Thessalonians 4:16, 17.

Paul calls the Christian's hope "that blessed hope, and the glorious appearing of the great God and our Saviour Jesus Christ." Titus 2:13.

The hope of the Christian depends on the second coming of our Lord, for He says, "Behold, I come quickly; and My reward is with Me, to give every man according as his work shall be." Revelation 22:12.

Yes, Jesus is coming again. And when He comes the righteous dead will be raised from their graves, and all that have been faithful and true will be rewarded with everlasting life in the paradise of God.

The reward is worth receiving. A beautiful crown is waiting; for Paul says, "Henceforth there is laid up for me a crown of righteousness, which the Lord, the righteous Judge, shall give me at that day; and not to me only, but unto all them also that love His appearing." 2 Timothy 4:6-8.

[194]

This is called a "crown of life," in James 1:12, and Revelation 2:10. Peter calls it a "crown of glory," and says it is to be given "when the Chief Shepherd shall appear." 1 Peter 5:4.

And this earth, cleansed and purified from sin and the effects of the curse, is to be our home. Peter says of it, "Nevertheless we, according to His promise, look for new heavens and a new earth, wherein dwelleth righteousness." 2 Peter 3:10, 13.

The New Jerusalem, which Christ is preparing in heaven, shall come down to earth and be its capital city. The apostle-prophet John said he "saw the holy city, New Jerusalem, coming down from God out of heaven."

"And I saw no temple therein; for the Lord God Almighty and the Lamb are the temple of it. . . . The Lamb is the light thereof. And the nations of them which are saved shall walk in the light of it."

"And God shall wipe away all tears from their eyes; and there shall be no more death, neither sorrow, nor crying, neither shall there be any more pain; for the former things are passed away."

"He that overcometh shall inherit all things; and I will be his God, and he shall be My son." Revelation 21:7.

The earth and the dominion of it were given to man at creation. These will be restored to him at redemption.

The prophet Micah said to the "daughter of Zion, unto thee shall it come, even the first dominion." Micah 4:8.

Then Eden lost will be Eden regained, and the lost dominion will be

The Dominion Restored
The Dominion Restored.

Made in the USA
Middletown, DE
30 August 2023

37630199R00036